GOING DOWN

JAYNE RYLON

OTHER BOOKS BY JAYNE RYLON

DIVEMASTERS
Going Down
Going Deep
Going Hard

MEN IN BLUE
Night is Darkest
Razor's Edge
Mistress's Master
Spread Your Wings
Wounded Hearts
Bound For You

POWERTOOLS
Kate's Crew
Morgan's Surprise
Kayla's Gift
Devon's Pair
Nailed to the Wall
Hammer it Home

HOTRODS
King Cobra
Mustang Sally
Super Nova
Rebel on the Run
Swinger Style
Barracuda's Heart

Touch of Amber
Long Time Coming

COMPASS BROTHERS

Northern Exposure
Southern Comfort
Eastern Ambitions
Western Ties

COMPASS GIRLS

Winter's Thaw
Hope Springs
Summer Fling
Falling Softly

PLAY DOCTOR

Dream Machine
Healing Touch

STANDALONES

4-Ever Theirs
Nice & Naughty
Where There's Smoke
Report For Booty

RACING FOR LOVE

Driven
Shifting Gears

RED LIGHT

Through My Window
Star

DEDICATION

For Mr. Rylon, who has sacrificed by traveling to each gorgeous setting in the Divemasters books even though he's afraid of flying, then explored them along with me to be sure my research was as thorough as possible. I know that was a tough job for you. ☺

You're the best SCUBA buddy a girl could ask for (except for that time you were sure my dive computer had gotten stolen when it was actually in your BCD pocket for the whole week of diving). I hope you enjoy the character I made you in this series...not that you read my books! But just in case, someday, you peek inside this one.

❧ ONE ❧

Archer Banks's ringing cell trampled the tropical night symphony composed of lulling waves, chirping bugs, and rustling palms. He would have fumbled around on the nightstand to silence the racket if an armful of bronzed, slender woman hadn't stopped him. After rolling the beach bunny off his chest, he settled her gently on the edge of his double bed. Refusing to be distracted by her wild, sun-bleached mane, or the way the moonlight streaming in the window highlighted her damn-near-perfect ass, he forced his dick's attention from the adorable snuffle she surrendered as she burrowed into his lumpy pillow.

Archer turned his back on all that natural beauty. He rebelled against everything in his soul by lunging instead for one of the only remnants of offensive technology he allowed to intrude in his life.

He didn't have a choice, really, since the hunk of plastic threatened the integrity of his eardrums by refusing to shut the fuck up.

Only one contact in the entire world had been programmed with the specific God-awful racket that now blared from his phone. The man who was instructed to interrupt Archer's solitude only in a life-or-death emergency.

Fuck. Fuck. Fuck.

Phone in hand, halfway unlocked, he launched himself from the freshly laundered sheets, which smelled of sunshine and ocean spray. He growled to the caller, "Don't expect me to rush to that bastard's side for some kind of deathbed confessional."

Archer figured he maybe should have said hello first. His bitterness had rushed out like pus from a festering wound before he could manage anything else. Odd, since he would have sworn these old injuries were scarred over by now.

"No need. He's gone." The familiar voice on the other end of the line, thousands of miles away, made Archer more homesick than the news of his own loss. "It was fast. Painless. Though probably traumatizing for the young ladies your father was attempting to have sex with when the stroke hit."

"Jesus." Archer stumbled across the room. He slipped out the sliding glass door that led to a half-rotten deck barely big enough for a pair of plastic chairs, then down the three steps to the beach. Naked, he sank onto his knees in the sand. He glanced over his shoulder toward the woman whose name wasn't nearly as memorable as the way she'd sucked him off before getting him hard again, then riding him with thighs powerful enough to cling to a breaching humpback.

Brittany! That was it. He was *almost* sure.

Was he turning into everything he'd spent his entire adult life trying to distance himself from? Had his father remembered the names associated with the assassin pussies that had finally managed to take the bastard out?

Archer's stomach churned at the thought. Acid seared his esophagus. Just like it had before he'd left that world he'd never belonged in. He hadn't looked back since. Not even for a glimpse of the girl he'd abandoned, who wouldn't welcome his attention after what had happened.

This was definitely going to be the second worst night of Archer's life.

"Sir?"

He shook his head when the question came softly—kindly, even—from his family's butler, who'd been more like a true relative than any Archer shared filthy blue blood with. It was the reason he'd borrowed the guy's name when he'd fled and remade himself. "Come on, Banks. You changed my shitty diapers plenty of times. Don't you think formality is uncalled for? I've never been that person. Much to my father's disappointment—"

"Archer." A soft chuckle warmed Banks's tone this time. "That might have been true once. But not always. Over time, I think he might have envied your escape. Admired it, though he was too proud to admit such things. Or maybe he respected you too much to go against your wishes and contact you to let you know."

"I highly doubt that." Archer swallowed hard against the feelings he'd thought he'd buried deeper than a pirate's treasure. He might be a thirty-one-year-old man, but some small part of him would always regret that he hadn't been able to be the son his father wanted.

"Well, this is for certain. He didn't truly disown you. You were never cut out of his will. In fact, despite your wishes, he left you everything."

"Shit! *Everything*?"

"His entire holdings. All of it, down to the last cent." Banks delivered the most devastating news of the night.

Everything Archer had never wanted had finally caught up with him. Golden chains ensnared his wrists and ankles, keeping him from imagining he could ever move freely again. He'd seen firsthand what it took to run an empire.

As quickly as a barracuda snaps up its unsuspecting dinner, Archer had gone from beach bum to billionaire.

Fuck him, life as he knew it—and *loved* it—was over.

He scrubbed his hands through his hair and caught sight of the woman he'd left in his bed dressing hurriedly by the light of the wall-mounted gooseneck lamp before blowing him a kiss and heading for the door.

At least he'd gone out with one hell of a bang.

Literally.

"It's not exactly a death sentence, sir."

"Banks," he growled.

"I mean...*Archie*."

The shock of hearing that long-lost nickname, right now, had Archer blinking fiercely. Somehow he didn't think there was enough salt in the air to blame his reaction on that. "It feels like it. I'm proud of who I am these days. I don't want the money. I don't want to be like him. I can't afford to lose myself."

He scrunched his eyes closed. It was as if he were a recovering alcoholic who'd been offered an entire chain of distilleries. Archer knew unimaginable wealth could corrupt him. It hadn't been easy to sacrifice everything once, but he'd quit superfluous material possessions cold turkey and had never been happier than he was here, with next to nothing.

Good friends, a job he loved, willing women, and time to enjoy life. Those things were priceless.

"So we'll give it away. Form an umbrella foundation that supports any number of charities, funds, and projects for worthwhile causes. A lot of problems can be solved with seven billion dollars, give or take." Banks's solution seemed genius. Simple yet complicated at the same time.

"Perfect. Will you help me? And by help me, I mean run it. Make the day-to-day decisions. I don't need to know the details. Use your judgment."

"Of course. If that's still what you want, after you've really thought about it some," Banks promised. "I am the estate's executor. It will take some time to settle things. Let me see to the legalities, and you start dreaming about who you'd like to help. This fortune could change the world."

"I...uh... Okay, thanks." Archer couldn't believe this was happening. "Name it after yourself. Call it the Banks Foundation."

He had to make sure his father's name wasn't included. No glory for that fucker.

"I suppose that's naming it after *us*, isn't it?" Banks sounded pleased with that. At least he didn't mind that Archer had appropriated his name in his attempt to go incognito.

"Make sure you pay yourself, too. A shit-ton. Ten times whatever you think is an outrageous salary. You deserve a hazard bonus for the decades you've put up with my family's shit. God knows I couldn't do it. As if that wasn't obvious when I bailed."

"I will." Banks laughed, then said warmly, "For the record, I'm proud of you, too. Dream big, Archie."

⌒ TWO ⌒

Only slightly after the ass crack of dawn, Archer blocked the past several sleepless hours from his mind. He verified the headcount of their boatload of guests for the morning's two-tank SCUBA dive. Then he began double-checking the equipment. Sticking to routine ensured he never missed anything vital. After all, it was his job to guarantee no one interrupted the fun-and-sun portion of their vacation by dying on his watch.

As he worked, he surreptitiously observed each of the three buddy pairs he'd be going down with. How they set up their gear was a decent indication of how they would dive. At least, he'd found that to be true in the past.

One couple, a husband and wife team, had stacked their gear neatly so that the first thing they'd need was on top and the last at the bottom. They spoke quietly as they worked seamlessly, assisting each other with their wet suits before unhurriedly progressing through their own personal buddy checklists. As he watched, they verified today's plans against their dive computers to ensure they wouldn't exceed their no-decompression limits given the nitrogen load they'd taken on in their shore dives the day before.

Of course, Archer had already done the same thing before they'd left the shop. Still, he was glad they were independent divers and didn't rely on his word for it.

They'd be fine.

Two brothers made up the second pair. They'd come to the dive shop yesterday afternoon asking plenty of questions about the boat, the tour size, the dive location, the depth of the sites they'd be visiting, typical currents in the area, notable marine life to look out for, and recent weather patterns. They had shared their religiously completed logbooks, which detailed over a hundred dives each, with the shop manager, too.

Archer wasn't worried about them either.

The third set of guests... He shook his head. There were a couple like them in every bunch.

True, the diving here in Bonaire—a fairly dinky desert island off the coast of Venezuela in the Southern Caribbean, next door to Aruba and Curaçao—was some of the easiest and most beautiful in the world. It made it a great spot for newbies to put some experience under their weight-belts. He didn't have any problem teaching the tadpoles good habits or helping them gain confidence in their emerging skills.

Unfortunately, this duo had enough experience to know better than some of the shit they were pulling already. They bickered, sniping at each other for losing this thing or that thing—extraneous, flashy doodads they probably didn't know how to use anyway. Their jumbled gear spilled across the modest thirty-six-foot boat's deck, causing Archer's fellow divemaster, Tosin, to have to dodge it as he helped his own half-dozen divers on the other side of the vessel. The problem children had already dunked their boots in the camera-and-regulator-only rinse tank before anyone could stop them.

Archer could also tell by the bulges of lead stuffing the pockets of their buoyancy control devices relative to their average builds that they were about to go overboard with far too much weight. Some was necessary to keep divers down. That much could be dangerous. He mentally prepared himself to grab for them if they overcompensated for their inevitable negative buoyancy at depth by puffing up their BCD's with an entire blimp's worth of air, which would expand on the ascent, rocketing them toward the surface as if they were helium balloons slipping free from a toddler's grasp.

Spending the day filling out incident reports and loading Mr. and Mrs. Yelly McYellington into a hyperbaric chamber after their lungs popped or they gave themselves the bends would not improve his pissy mood.

He kept trying to pretend today was exactly like the past 4,380 other days—give or take some—he'd done pretty much the same thing as this. Pencil lead snapped when he pressed too hard against his ratty clipboard mid check-off.

"Rough night?" Miguel winked as he took his place at the boat's helm and curled his fingers around the wheel. Though he was the third divemaster onboard this morning, it was his turn to drive. He'd stay on the surface, assist any divers who aborted early for mechanical, health, or safety concerns, and make sure nobody surfside bothered their stuff.

Things could be worse, Archer acknowledged. At least he'd get to dive today.

He grunted. "You have no idea."

Nor would they any time soon. Discussing serious personal matters in front of their clients was a no-no. Besides, he had to find the right time to come clean to his best friends about his sordid past.

They pushed off the dock and headed through the muted peach-and-rose post-dawn for Klein Bonaire, an *exceptionally* dinky uninhabited blob of land less than a mile offshore from the main island. Protected by the curvature of Bonaire, it held plenty of opportunities for excursions. Most of the guests went shore diving on their own when unguided. The guys preferred to take them somewhere they couldn't reach in the rusty white mini pick-up trucks that came standard with their condo rentals.

"She did look like a wild catch, you lucky bastard," Tosin joked from where he meticulously verified everyone's equipment set-up. Another set of eyes. He had their backs. Just like Archer and Miguel would have his. Focused, he thankfully didn't read too much into Archer's lack of a response. He turned on tanks, checked air pressure gauges, and helped a few people with rental gear clip their neon-yellow secondary regulators to the proper place for easy access in case anything went haywire with their primary.

Considering the three of them also serviced the equipment at the shop they currently worked for, Archer didn't think that was likely. Never hurt to have a spare, though. Especially when you were more than a breath's worth of a swim from the surface and counted on it to deliver your air supply.

Twelve guests, two divemasters, and one captain.

Archer, Tosin, and Miguel had worked for operations that ran much bigger ratios of clients to guides, but they preferred not to. This way they could make sure everyone had a safe, personalized experience.

Today, Archer's group would be staying shallower than Tosin's. That meant he had the less experienced people. Or in the case of his married couple, ones who preferred nicer light for capturing the best underwater photos and videos. The brothers had chosen a depth that would allow them to stay under the longest. Another smart choice, Archer thought.

If he only had a few days a year or every couple of years to dive while on vacation, he'd milk every one of them, too. Sounded like hell to him.

Different priorities for different folks. Everyone had their own reasons for the decisions they made. No different than him. At least that's what he promised himself to assuage his guilt for not being honest with his two best friends about his life before they'd started exploring paradises together nearly a dozen years earlier. Twice for not telling them about how everything had changed overnight.

He'd confess...eventually. When he could convince himself that it didn't matter and wouldn't impact the partnership they'd built. Part of him screamed that wouldn't be possible, not when he told them about the worst of it. About the unforgivable thing he'd done to *her*.

Archer couldn't help himself. A vision of a young woman with hair fanned out around her and gorgeous eyes looking up at him as he made love to her flashed into his mind. It simultaneously turned him on and made him feel sick.

So he ignored any further ribbing from Miguel and Tosin. Let them think what they would. Sure, his date had wrung a few solid orgasms from him, but he'd already practically forgotten about that. God knew he could use a few more to relax him now.

What would he do if this whole existence disappeared? If he had to go back, he'd bleach out and die off like coral in ever-warming ocean waters. He wouldn't be able to survive in those conditions.

Archer gripped the edge of the cabin and stuck his face into the wind, closing his eyes as he savored the strengthening sunrays and the salt spray pelting his cheeks. He wasn't ready to let go.

Not now.

Not ever.

Miguel interrupted his wandering thoughts with a low warning. "Archer, behind you."

He snapped around, searching for the problem.

Married couple had finished getting ready. Without distractions, people sometimes had too much time on their hands. It seemed that was the case today, as they skimmed across the surface of the water toward their destination.

Another common occurrence.

"Need help?" He forced himself to smile as he approached the pair. Crouching down, he held on to the rinse tank at the center of the boat to keep his balance on the moving vessel.

"Sorry, I get nervous. Every time." The wife swiped at a stray lock, putting it right back where it had started for only a millisecond before a gust slapped it over her eyes once more. Glamour had no place in diving. Skin-tight suits, wind-blown hair, an odd assortment of UV protection—hats, oversized sunglasses, rash guards—and mismatched towels. That's what he considered their uniform.

Functional. Not too pretty. Definitely informal. Exactly the way he liked things.

Archer wondered if Banks would work some magic and keep him from having to wear an entirely different kind of suit for the first time in a decade. Or, God forbid, a tux. Could the man really pull off the legal and financial shit without dragging Archer back to the States in person?

Lost in thought, he hesitated too long in reassuring his charge. She'd progressed to biting her lip as her husband squeezed her knee. His friends had him covered as usual, though.

Tosin piped up. "No worries. If you don't do this every day, it's easy to get rusty. But you'll be diving with the best. I guarantee when you put your mask in the water and take a peek at the reef below you, your nerves will disappear. Besides, Archer is willing to hold your hand the whole way if you need some extra reassurance."

Great, he didn't need his ass kicked by a jealous husband today. Usually they saved that line for the single ladies. And meant it. Diving with a woman was probably the most intimate experience he'd ever had with one. Fortunately, this husband chuckled, confident in his bond with his wife and seemingly grateful for the divemasters putting her at ease.

Archer wondered what it would be like to have that sort of relationship.

He, Tosin, and Miguel had never stayed in one place long enough to try. Being pinned down like that sounded like torture, except for one or two things—

like, say, decent home cooking—they might be missing out on. It had seemed like an easy sacrifice before.

Suddenly, he was second-guessing everything.

Damn his father.

Even from the grave, the bastard had the power to fuck with Archer's head.

Tosin gave him a kick in the ass.

Nervous lady. Right. Archer shook his head, probably making his dark hair stick up worse than it already had been. He didn't give a shit about that. "Tosin's right. You're prepared. I watched you set up. Why don't we go over the dive plan as a group?"

Head in the game once more, he gathered his six charges around and spoke loudly enough to be heard over the engine. "This is going to be a nice and easy dive at one of our favorite sites, Knife. The boat will be moored in about fifteen feet of water. Sandy bottom. We're going to head out over the ridge of the reef, where the sea floor begins to slope down. I'll drop to about fifty feet or so and judge the current. It's usually going east from here, so we'll likely turn right, keeping the reef on that side of us. Stay with your buddies, wherever you're comfortable. I'll be using a very conservative profile. As long as you let me be the deepest person on the dive and the farthest ahead, you'll be all set, even if you aren't confident in reading your computers or the battery goes out or whatever."

He'd added that last part for his problematic pair.

"Whoever hits eighteen-hundred PSI first will signal to me using the half-tank sign." As a reminder, Archer demonstrated, putting one hand up and the other across the top so that it made something like a T. "At that point, the whole group will turn around. We'll ascend—*slowly.*"

Extra pointed stare at the disaster duo there.

Unfortunately, they were digging around in their pockets, not paying attention.

"Stay around twenty to thirty feet deep and put the reef on your left for the return swim. The current will be in our favor, helping us back to the boat with less exertion in a shorter amount of time. Plus, the decreased pressure at the shallower depth will ensure we make it there with plenty of air left. Feel free to use it to explore the area beneath the boat. Tosin and Miguel spotted a seahorse and a frogfish in that exact location last week. We may get lucky. I'll be sure to point out anything of interest so you can take pictures or come in for a closer look.

"When you're down to about eight hundred pounds of air, I'll send you up to the base of the boat's mooring line to do your safety stop. Stay for three minutes at fifteen feet. Your computer will count it down for you. Then ascend nice and easy to the boat. Miguel will be waiting to help you out. As always, please remember this is a protected marine reserve. Do not touch anything. Keep your distance from the reef, especially the soft corals. Don't harass the animals. And definitely leave only bubbles behind."

With a plan in place, his nervous diver seemed more relaxed. Good thing, since they'd reached the mooring pin. A buoy connected by a line to a concrete slab carefully placed on the sea floor allowed the boat to stay in one place without dropping an anchor that could tear up the reef.

Miguel and Tosin were securing a rope to the mooring pin. Archer checked his tank one last time, ducked into his BCD, snapped himself in, tightened the straps, and headed for the platform at the back of the boat. His gear seemed heavier than usual. Or maybe he was simply off balance. He hated to admit, even to himself, that he might be reeling from the news Banks had given him.

He slipped on his fins and mask then waited for the all clear from Miguel. When his friend flashed the sign, Archer turned to his group and said, "I'll be waiting in the water when you're ready. Miguel will help you if you need anything prior to entry."

Tosin's group of more advanced divers were already giant striding into the ocean and bobbing behind the boat, talking excitedly about how clear the water was and what they might see. A few were hoping to catch a lionfish for dinner. The species wasn't indigenous to the Caribbean and had been devouring juvenile fish on the reef, so it was open hunting season. Malicious and delicious, as the locals liked to describe them.

With a final glance over his shoulder and a nod from Miguel, Archer put one hand on his mask, the other over his regulator, then took a single step out into the ocean.

A curtain of bubbles rose around him as he plummeted a few feet below the cerulean surface. He loved the moment he became part of the sea again. The puff of air he'd added to his BCD before entering lifted him enough that his head stuck out of the water, though, as he waited for his guests to join him.

One by one, they splooshed into the water.

When all six of his charges were huddled around, peeking at the hidden world below their dangling flippers, he asked, "Who's ready to go down?"

He flashed the thumbs-down. In return, he received an okay gesture from most of his divers. Of course, the sixth one—part of his trouble couple— shot back a thumbs-up. In diving language that meant "ascend", not "awesome". He shook his head and the diver corrected himself, changing to an okay instead.

With that, Archer popped his regulator back in, held his deflator hose up with his left hand, dumped the air from his BCD, and began to descend. Water filled his ears and closed over his head as he entered the magical universe beneath the surface. At least for an hour or so, he could forget his worries.

Had to, in order to do his job right.

These folks trusted him with their lives. He'd never lost a diver yet, and didn't plan to start today. Sure, they were only fifty-three feet below the surface of the Caribbean Sea.

Still plenty deep enough to drown.

That wouldn't be happening on his watch. If nothing else, he was certain of one thing.

He was a damn fine divemaster.

THREE

A month later, Archer did a lazy frog kick, propelling himself through the warm, blue ocean. Tosin was a few feet to his right and Miguel a bit ahead of them as he peered at the shoal of squids that hovered in the shallows nearby. Their fins fluttered along the length of their bodies like a girl's skirt ruffling in the wind. They changed colors and textures as their tentacles waved, flashing some sort of mesmerizing message the humans in their midst couldn't decipher.

Though they'd seen these animals or ones like them many times before, the cephalopods still fascinated Archer. His friends, too.

Sure, it was their day off. That didn't keep them out of the water.

Instead, they got to enjoy their time below the surface instead of worrying about anyone else. Miguel and Tosin were plenty capable of taking care of themselves. So was he. They glided offshore from Windsock, a dive site they visited often. It got its name from the device at the end of the island's runway, which was right across the street from the beach where they'd made their shore entry for today's excursion.

Though they normally set an easy pace on their guided dives so that the tourists who'd hired them could keep up while gawking at the marine life surrounding them, today they progressed even more slowly. Deep, measured respiration maximized their bottom time. It also forced Archer to chill out for a while—a skill he seemed to have lost any time he wasn't underwater lately.

Despite the fact that they'd already been down more than an hour, they hadn't covered nearly as much ground as they did when they were escorting passing visitors through as much of the aquatic landscape as possible.

Keen eyes, trained, could pick out any number of curiosities less experienced divers would zip right past, none the wiser. Like the lobster hiding beneath a vase sponge at depth, or the seahorse clinging to a swaying soft coral a few hundred feet back, or the teeny Pederson cleaner shrimp nestled in an anemone. They went about their business less than three feet from his face right then.

Each thing he saw awed him, as if it were his first time witnessing the splendor of this environment. Down here, Archer's troubles couldn't eclipse his wonder.

The only other time he experienced a rush this intense followed by contentment this profound was during an epic fuck. Just like then, no matter how hard he tried, he couldn't make it last forever. Too soon, regret rushed in. When compared to the single night he'd spent with the girl whose name he couldn't bear to think—even to himself—every other experience paled, even if it made him a sick fuck to admit it.

Tosin clinked a carabiner against his tank a couple times. When he had their attention, he flashed his low-air signal. Together, the three of them turned toward the shore and made their way to the outcropping of fire coral they used as their safety stop marker when they dove here.

Those final 180 seconds ticked by in a flash. Literally, as Archer watched the lacey reflections of the powerful sun dancing across the sea floor. They lit up the electric blue spots and fluorescent yellow tail on the juvenile damselfishes peeking out from between the blades below him.

How many of them would survive long enough to thrive on the reef? Despite their best attempts at hiding, the majority would be gobbled up by something higher on the food chain before they could fully mature.

He wondered if his odds were even half as good as the ones dealt to the fingerlings, who darted into some hidden nook when Archer's shadow passed over them.

After their countdown completed, they followed each other single-file through a channel in the coral, over a bed of rubble. Archer's computer marked each foot they rose, from fifteen to five. Before he was ready to rejoin the realm of land-lovers, his head crested the surface.

"Did you see how that thing almost ran into me?" Miguel was pumped over his close encounter with the squid.

"It was awesome. I could see the surface of its skin changing colors and my own reflection in its eyeball. Lucky it didn't hypnotize me or some shit!" Tosin joined in.

Usually, the first moments above water bubbled over with excited chatter as everything they'd been thinking rushed out once they regained the ability to speak. Sure, they had perfected their own version of sign language, and carried slates to write notes to each other when that wouldn't suffice, but nothing beat talking about their discoveries.

Today, Archer had nothing to contribute.

The whole world had flipped upside down. Dropping his regulator and taking his first breath of air from the atmosphere, he suddenly felt like he was drowning.

He sighed as he braced himself against the waves in thigh-deep water, then tugged on the spring straps of his fins, completing his transformation from merman to stealth billionaire. A guy he wasn't sure he wanted to be anymore.

With one final glance over his shoulder, he ducked his head and trailed behind his friends.

They trundled through the gentle surf toward the beach. Salt water sluiced off him, making his footprints in the sand turn dark and clumpy. He relished the burn in his calves and thighs as he hauled himself and his sixty-plus pounds of equipment up the unstable incline, over rocks and past cacti, until they reached their truck, parked at the side of the road.

No need for a gym membership when this was part of their daily regime. Sometimes they did as many as five dives in a day. Often they followed it up with some midnight cardio that worked entirely different sets of muscles. Exhausting, but he'd never gotten sick of it.

Miguel rested his tank on the tailgate as he slipped off his mask, then unsnapped from his BCD. "If you guys will break down my stuff, I'll go get in line at the street-meat stand."

Fish from a roadside tin can? Guaranteed food poisoning, right?

Archer had been skeptical once, too.

Now he knew better than to listen to his inner snob.

The place served the freshest fish, caught daily, and had become a staple of their diet since they'd landed on the tarmac not too far from where he stood. Hard to believe that had only been a few short months ago.

If their patterns held true, it wouldn't be too much longer before one of them got a tip on another destination looking for help. Someone who'd be downright giddy to take on a trio of divemasters with their credentials. Off they'd go again.

Who knew where they'd end up next?

Well, he actually had some idea. But would the guys be onboard? Would they come onboard?

Archer screwed the dust cap onto his regulator and finished neatly arranging their gear so they could dunk it in the freshwater bins back at the resort before retiring to the tiny cabanas provided for each of the staff members in an attempt to justify their ridiculously low wages.

Honestly, he wasn't in any hurry to return. He hadn't been able to sleep much recently. Every time he closed his eyes, dreams of her turned into a nightmare replay of the situation that had driven him to leave it all behind. Another night of staring at the bamboo ceiling might push him over the edge of his sanity. Tosin and Miguel went out a lot of nights, or were otherwise occupied, so he'd spent a lot of time alone lately.

He snagged their pile of blankets then headed back to the beach. Lizards scattered in front of him, and a kickass blue whiptail sunned itself on the yellow-and-black painted rock that marked the location of the dive site along the way. More than sixty of those helpful stones dotted the shores of Bonaire, which was truly one of the most SCUBA-friendly places they'd ever lived and worked.

Had they visited every single site on the island yet? He'd have to check the marine park map tucked into his logbook tonight, and speed up the process if they hadn't. They couldn't have much time left. A week at most, he figured.

Maybe the impending shakeup made him clingy, since Archer found himself nostalgic for once. Curious, since they'd been places so lush and green they almost hurt to look at. Somehow, he'd fallen in love with the deserts of Bonaire, the donkeys that wandered into the road and blocked traffic, and the one-way roads on the north side of the island that forced you to do a tour of the lake just to get back to town. He couldn't get enough of watching the world-class kite surfers on Lac Bay, kayaking through the mangroves, exploring the caves complete with ancient paintings, or hanging out in the blustery gusts on the wild east side...next stop, Africa. Even the salt fields where the locals pumped water onto the land—no good for anything else, certainly not growing anything edible—to evaporate it and sell the sea salt left behind seemed charming when they were dotted with grazing flamingos. And the salt pier where the goods were put on giant ships was one of the coolest places to dive under and around, always teeming with tarpon, groupers, and schools of barracudas.

People in Bonaire made the best of everything they'd been given. Like he, Tosin, and Miguel had done.

He remembered the adventures they'd had together so far instead of looking forward to whatever came next. If things worked out like Banks kept assuring him it would, maybe they could return someday. Here or to any of the other places they'd discovered on their journey around the world.

Tosin dropped a cooler full of beer onto the sand between the blankets Archer had only barely finished spreading over the crushed coral. He rubbed his bare abs above the shorts he'd tugged on to conceal his European-style trunks. "I'm starving."

"Nothing new there." Archer snorted.

"Hey, all that swimming makes a man hungry." Tosin practically drooled. "Besides, I burned off a ton of calories last night with the gorgeous Asian woman we met in the market a couple days ago."

"Aki?" Archer prided himself on recalling her name along with the lilac bikini that hadn't concealed her outstanding rack.

"Sounds right. Why? You didn't already do her and forget to mention it, did you?" Tosin squinted at Archer. He glanced away, pretending to stare at the waves kissing the shore. His friend misinterpreted his awkwardness. "Wait, you didn't call dibs and I forgot—?"

They may have been players, but even they had their own code between them. *No poaching* being one of the cardinal rules that had kept them from having a major falling out these past twelve years.

"Nah, nothing like that. Just...an unusual name. Pretty."

"I guess. Not as pretty as some other things about her, though." Tosin shrugged. "Anyway, it was her last night in town. She showed up at my door, so I helped her make some sexy memories for her scrapbook."

Lucky for the hungry horndog, Miguel was heading back, his arms piled with takeout containers.

Archer promised himself he'd put away every morsel of his. Not only because he could see the chalkboard bolted to the side of the truck. Lionfish—his favorite—was the special of the day.

It seemed a month of freaking out every moment he wasn't underwater had started to take its toll. He'd mooned an entire boatload of divers the day before when his trunks had refused to hug his hips no matter how hard he yanked on the tie that cinched the waist. The straps on his BCD couldn't get any tighter either.

He rubbed the back of his neck.

"Still not sleeping well?" Tosin asked.

"There are probably better mattresses in prison than my bunkhouse. Or maybe I'm getting old. Creaky. Probably should make an appointment for a massage or something." That was no lie. He practically got a cramp in his knotted shoulder muscles as he tried to shrug off his friend's concern before Miguel could wander into hearing range and start hounding him again.

Too late.

"What you need is to get your dick sucked," Miguel ribbed Archer as he passed out orders, slinging his shaggy hair out of his eyes with a whip of his head.

"You offering?" He kicked some sand in the asshole's direction, knowing that wasn't his intention.

"Hell no." Miguel snorted. "That new brunette working the fryer wrote her number on a napkin and asked me to give it to you, though. I'm pretty sure you could pretend I forgot your fork and have that food cart rocking before I finish my salad. Be careful you don't set any important bits on fire while you're at it, though."

"Not interested." Archer shook his head. Now, if she'd had black hair and blue eyes, maybe he could have pretended it meant something long enough for his dick to get hard.

Tosin and Miguel exchanged stares for a little too long.

"What?" he asked.

"Look, I don't want to get up in your business, but...what the hell is going on?" Tosin demanded as he tore into a mountain of garlic shrimp. "She's your type. Tall, athletic, tan. Natural. Down to fuck. If she doesn't do it for you, no one will. And you haven't taken a woman home in weeks."

A month, Archer mentally corrected.

Miguel jumped in when Tosin ran out of steam. Or needed another bite of his dinner. Priorities, people. "I can't remember you ever having a dry spell like this before. Did you break your dick? Catch something? What? Come on, we won't laugh...much. Tell us."

Archer grimaced. "You're idiots. Both of you."

"*You're* dodging. Is he right, then? You're clearing up a case of the clap or something?" Tosin's eyes narrowed as he thought back, as if trying to figure out when Archer might have snuck off to the botika for a shot of antibiotics in the ass.

"Jesus, no." He groaned. "My junk is fine, okay? It's just that I've been thinking a lot lately."

About mistakes he'd made, and how he might fix them going forward. About her. About holding out for someone who might make him feel like she used to or, at least, something close.

"*Thinking*! What the fuck you doing that for, bro?" Miguel chided with a smirk as he inhaled another piece of grilled barracuda from between his fingers.

Tosin agreed, "Dumb idea."

"Tell me about it." A grimace crossed Archer's face. He had to give them something or they'd keep hounding him. Besides, maybe it was time to dip a toe in and see how they might react. "I guess I'm starting to wonder if there should be more to life."

"More than great sex, diving, and hanging out at the beach with your friends?" Tosin spread his arms, still clutching some shrimp between his thumb and forefinger.

Archer picked at his lionfish nuggets, which suddenly seemed like a mountain of a meal. "Yeah."

"You're worse off than if you *had* caught some crotch funk." Miguel stopped and stared. "This has been our goal for the past dozen years. Doing exactly what we love until we get bored and move to the next gorgeous place where we can start exploring all over again. Haven't we always said we're the luckiest bastards in the world?"

He nodded. "We *are*. We totally are. We've travelled around the globe, seen incredible things—"

"Given lady tourists the vacation fling of a lifetime," Miguel added with an exaggerated jab or two of a French fry topped with Dutch mayo sauce.

Archer probably would have laughed if what he wanted to say wasn't so serious. "What if we're capable of something equally awesome and more meaningful?"

"Hey, it may not be brain surgery or ending hunger, but I think showing people the time of their lives underwater or in my bed is a valuable contribution to society. And I also happen to enjoy it. Thoroughly." Tosin pounded himself on the chest.

He did have a reputation for pleasing his partners. Hell, each of them did.

"You're right." Archer choked down another tasteless bite of what was usually his favorite meal. Then he slammed the rest of his beer, as if that would soothe his parched throat.

"Don't bail on us now, Archer." Miguel frowned. "We're a team. This is what we do, who we are. Divemasters. That's always been good enough before."

"It still is," he was quick to reassure them. "Always will be. Forget I said anything."

"Sure." Tosin nodded so fast he might have given himself whiplash. On their previous day off, he'd leapt from the cliffs at Boca Slagbaai without thinking twice. He probably found that a million times less daunting than this heartfelt discussion they were stumbling through.

Before things could deteriorate into some sloppy show of their devotion to their best friends, Miguel lightened the mood. Right when Archer went to wipe his hands on his napkin, his friend dove forward, snatching it from his grasp. Then he crashed into the sand, holding the scrap of recycled paper aloft in his fist.

"Waste not, want not. Since you're not interested..."

"Go for it." Archer laughed. The hottie—he'd learn her name tomorrow, he promised himself—*had* caught his eye. Beautiful and carefree, she might have tempted him if he hadn't decided that sex should involve something more than a temporary endorphin rush from now on. It would be another way to distinguish himself from his father. Besides, he knew from experience that as great as casual sex was, it had nothing on sleeping with someone whose top three attributes were something greater than her tits, her ass, and her willingness to give him a blowjob.

Although that last one might be a keeper, the other two should probably be shit like shared interests or a similar sense of humor.

Archer hadn't allowed himself to believe he'd have another shot at a genuine connection like that in his lifetime. Or maybe he'd been too scared to find it, only to fuck it up royally. Again.

Miguel returned from getting seconds he didn't really need just to chat some more with the cute young kite surfer slash food truck worker. He splayed on the sand like a beached whale and let out a world-class belch. "I'm never eating again."

"Yeah, sure." Tosin laughed. "You know you say that like twice a week, right?"

"I mean it. At least until breakfast." He grinned. "But I don't plan to move from this spot for a while."

"Fine by me." Archer could listen to the waves for hours as he watched iguanas scamper through the dusty soil or up the divi divi trees surrounding their oasis. Soon the sun would set. Then maybe they'd start a fire and hang out under the stars as they had plenty of other times.

Close to Kralendijk, the largest town on Bonaire, they had a great view of the comings and goings from the island's main harbor. A departing cruise ship shrank on the horizon as her thousands of passengers prepared to invade and overwhelm the port at their next destination.

Focused on the pair of tugboats returning to their stations after helping the ship out to sea, Archer didn't realize there was another large vessel on the horizon at first.

"Wow. Check that out." Miguel practically purred as he drew Archer and Tosin's attention to the incoming megayacht.

Archer's stomach churned. He slapped the lid of his takeout box closed. So much for that.

He swallowed hard as he studied the sleek profile of the ship, more impressive than he remembered. This was it. His time had run out.

Please, let him have done the right thing.

Tosin stood, shielding his eyes against the lowering sun for a better view. "It's gotta be over two-hundred feet. We might not be the luckiest bastards in the world after all. Imagine the guy who can afford something like that. Damn."

Archer didn't have to. "She's actually 273 feet long. Has room for a crew of sixteen plus twenty-five guests comfortably. Specialized dive platforms, two rigid-hull inflatable boats, and gear areas. A pool, medical center, fitness and rec room, three sun decks, pretty much anything you can think of."

"You know that boat?" Miguel squinted, as if he could read the name freshly painted on the bow. It wouldn't have mattered. This vessel wasn't one they'd seen in a past port they'd visited.

"Yep. She's mine," Archer admitted, then prayed he wasn't about to destroy the best thing he'd ever had.

Their friendship.

∽ FOUR ∾

Miguel and Tosin cracked up. Tosin shoved Archer's shoulder, toppling him into the sand beside the blanket. "You own a megayacht. Right. You had me going for a minute there, asshole."

Archer shrugged, dusted himself off, then figured he might as well start playing his cards. If he wasn't about to crap his trunks, it might even be kind of fun to see their reactions once they realized he wasn't fucking with them after all.

"What if it was true, though?" Archer pressed on. "Imagine that instead of jamming our stuff into a beat-up old duffle bag and taking off from here, we never had to pack again. We'd each have our own cabin onboard. A permanent home that moves with us. One a hell of a lot nicer than the places we've stayed before, too."

Archer wasn't referring to the marble and teak finishes the staterooms boasted. He meant the plush beds, world-class diving facilities, and the gorgeous natural light that would pour through the large cabin windows. The ability to go anywhere, anytime they felt like it. Those luxuries he could get behind, though Miguel and Tosin might not reject opulence for the sake of it like he did.

The guys started to get in on it then, making Archer's jaw unclench just a little. Miguel leaned back, knitted his fingers together, and let his hands rest on his washboard abs, still flat despite how much he'd gorged. "Hell yeah. We could run charters and escort rich people around the world. Show them the places we've discovered. Make a killing while we're at it."

"We could." Archer cleared his throat. "Or...since, you know, we'd have to be rich enough to take golden dumps to own a yacht like that, we could let people come along for free. Figure out some way to invite remarkable and deserving guests to join us on an all-expenses-paid trip of a lifetime. Use our matching private jet to shuttle them to wherever we're docked and go from there. Make people's dreams come true. Only fair since we'd get to live ours."

"I like that way better." Tosin nodded. "Like some kind of seafaring Willy Wonka."

Archer snorted. Only his dumbass friend would put it like that. Except, now that he had... "Yeah! We'd send out golden tickets or some shit, maybe sometimes auction off spots then donate the money to charities. Even better would be if there was a club on board so we could socialize. A place where people could unwind at night and make sure we're never lonely out on the open ocean. Not that different from what we do today, just at a whole different level."

"Now you're talking." Miguel grunted. "Make it a sex club—a hedonistic one like the places we went to in the Philippines—while you're at it. I'll sign up right now."

"Seriously?" Archer held his breath.

"Yeah, I mean, do I look dumb?" He whipped his head around to stare at Archer. "Saying no to a gig like that would be as idiotic as you turning down prime pussy. Oh, wait...fucking moron."

Unable to drag things out anymore, Archer asked, "Want to drive into town and watch her dock up close?"

"Sure. Maybe we can offer our services for a day or two if they're staying until Wednesday," Tosin suggested, referring to their next day off. "Hell, I'd volunteer just to score a tour. I bet that thing is ridiculous inside."

It was.

"We'd better hurry. She's fast. Must have a lot of horsepower below deck." Tosin had already climbed to his feet, scooped up his blanket, and lifted the cooler to his shoulder. Miguel and Archer were right behind.

It only took them a few minutes to navigate the roundabout and the narrow, cluttered streets of Kralendijk. They parked island-style, halfway on the brick sidewalk near the market, which was rapidly emptying of vendors now that the cruise ship had departed.

"Come on," Archer called to his friends as he unbuckled himself and headed for the dock. His anticipation grew, muffling some of his anxiety. The yacht was truly gorgeous. Sleek and modern. Not normally what attracted him. This time, he knew what that exterior held, though. He couldn't wait to catch a glimpse of the hardwood decks or the elaborate diving setups he'd instructed Banks to arrange. Not to mention seeing the man himself.

Archer admitted he'd missed the guy, especially after working covertly with him the past several weeks to approve the establishment of the Banks Foundation and start outlining some of the programs it would support, like the one he was about to pitch to his friends. Banks had been the person Archer had always chosen to go to when he was growing up—for help, to confide in, for approval. His younger self's judgment had been bang on. Banks was one of the good ones.

He'd made good time. The weather must not have been as bad as expected for their Atlantic crossing. Banks had cleaned house, hiring a brand-new crew that was aligned with Archer's mission for the *Divemaster.* Then he'd overseen renovations and transporting the yacht from where it had been docked in the Mediterranean for years, hardly ever used by Archer's father, who'd only commissioned one of the biggest ships in the world because he could, and because he couldn't stand for his associates or competitors to have something he didn't.

That's not at all what this was about for Archer.

"You coming?" he asked when Miguel put his arm up along the back of the seat and stared wistfully out the window.

"Our gear is in the back." Miguel sighed. "I'll stay with the truck. You two can check it out."

Archer shook his head. Hell, let someone take their stuff. He'd already arranged for upgraded equipment—the top-of-the-line products each guy had drooled over in catalogs—to be onboard. "I'll cover it up. It'll be okay for a minute or two. We can see the lot from there."

Archer rearranged the blankets to obscure their things.

"Not smart, but screw it. Let's do it." Tosin could never resist an adventure. Even unwise ones.

Maybe this was going to work out like Banks kept promising it would.

Miguel rounded the bed of the truck, joining them on the sidewalk. He pointed at the ship's hull as they jogged down the dock. "Hey, cool! She's called the *Divemaster*."

"Then I guess they probably won't be needing us." Tosin damn near pouted, as if someone had just broken the news to him that he'd missed something rare on a dive, like the enormous whale shark Archer and Miguel had glimpsed on their final shift in Útila.

"Don't rule it out yet," Archer mumbled as they closed in.

They arrived at the end of the pier around the same time a deckhand maneuvered a motorized gangway into place. Archer didn't bother to take a seat on the heavy-duty chain strung between two pilings like his friends did. Instead, he stood near the metal railing and waved at the man waiting at the other end of the bridge between Archer's past and his future.

"Good afternoon, Archie." Banks smiled and extended his hand as he glided down the gangway, as sophisticated as ever.

Archer skipped formality and used the grip to pull Banks in for a hug, earning a surprised grunt from the guy. It didn't take long before Banks reciprocated with a tender pat on Archer's shoulder blade. When they separated, Archer realized Banks had a hell of a lot more silver in his hair than the last time Archer had seen him, over a decade ago.

What differences would Banks notice about him? Pretty much everything, he figured. A ton more than a couple of grays.

He found it impossible to know what to say. If Banks was shocked, he masked it well.

Tosin and Miguel, however, were exchanging bug-eyed glances while Tosin mouthed, *Archie? What the fuck?*

Banks to the rescue again. Social niceties were his business. "This must be Mr. Torres and Mr. Ellis. I've heard so many wonderful things about you both."

Too dumbstruck to respond, first Miguel then Tosin took Banks's hand and shook woodenly before Tosin turned to Miguel and asked, "Is someone punking us right now?"

In sync, they looked around as if a camera crew would pop out from behind a rock to deliver the punch line of this joke.

For the first time in a month, Archer laughed. Once he started, he couldn't stop. He grabbed his middle then doubled over, relief and terror mingling, threatening to drive him mad.

"Why don't you invite your friends onboard, Archie?" Banks nudged him when he gasped to catch his breath. "There's a lot to discuss still, yes?"

That sobered him pretty quick. He nodded.

"I've set up a table for you in the bar, unless you'd prefer one of the decks or a meeting room instead." Banks had thought of everything Archer found overwhelming. As usual.

Tosin hadn't moved. "I think maybe you'd better introduce us first, *Archie*."

"Ah, shit. Sorry. I never was good at manners." He shook his head ruefully. Other than stating his name, there was no way to explain who this man was to Archer. Confidant, surrogate dad, business manager—he played a lot of roles. So he stuck with simplicity. "This is Banks."

"Wait. What?" Miguel tipped his head. Not surprising since that was Archer's alias and he now shared it with the other guy he so obviously knew. "I thought you didn't have any family."

"Technically, we're not related, sir," Banks replied for him.

"Sir!" Tosin snorted, recovering some of his easygoing nature, or maybe he attempted to counterbalance Miguel's growing agitation. "That's a first. Even better than Archie!"

"These guys are my friends, Banks. They're not going to respond to civility any better than I do." Archer looked away from Miguel when he realized the man had, consciously or not, balled his fists. It was entirely possible Archer would get his ass kicked today. And deserve it, too.

"Very well, then." Banks smiled and turned his back. "Get your asses onboard if you want to find out what the hell your friend is up to. Please leave your shoes in the bin at the top of the gangway."

Tosin whooped and raced onto the ship, excited to check it out despite the mysterious circumstances.

"I'd better not." Miguel frowned. "Our gear is in the truck, unattended. And I'm starting to think I'm the only one here who hasn't lost his damn mind."

Before he could come up with another valid reason to disappear, maybe forever, Banks dispatched a crew member toward the vehicle they'd left haphazardly on the curb nearby. "Your belongings will be safe. I promise."

"Holy shit. You've got to see this pool, Miguel. Come on!" Tosin shouted from the main sundeck.

Miguel grunted, then grudgingly followed, glancing over his shoulder periodically at Archer, who brought up the rear.

At least he was going to give Archer a chance to explain.

That was as much as he had dared to hope for.

Archer pinched the bridge of his nose, hoping he hadn't initiated a countdown sequence that led to the implosion of their friendship.

FIVE

Banks graciously asked the men, "Would you like a tour of the ship?"

"Hell yeah." Tosin practically vibrated as he looked around.

Archer hoped he'd be equally excited when he learned that the *Divemaster* could be his new home.

"Hang on. No." Miguel glared directly at Archer, as if he had blinders on—or didn't want to be softened up by their surroundings. "Not until we know what the fuck is going on here."

He was smart.

Archer didn't blame him at all. He gave a curt nod then said to Banks, "Show us to the bar, please."

"The papers you requested are at your place," Banks murmured as he guided them through a fiberglass door.

Even Archer was impressed when he took in the wide polished-wood hallway with calm, neutral-toned accents. He suspected Banks had done more than change out the crew onboard and make minor updates. Everything suited his tastes to perfection. Masculine, earthy, and understated elegance. Not a single garish embellishment lingered to remind him of his father.

Quietly, he asked Banks, "How'd you manage to redecorate so quickly?"

"Everything is possible with enough money, Archie." He winked.

They didn't have time to argue about that before they'd reached their destination near the bow of the ship. Floor-to-ceiling windows, contoured to the ship's silhouette, lined every edge of the room, giving them an unobstructed view of the harbor and northward along the western shore of the island. Klein Bonaire looked close enough to swim to from here.

It took Archer's breath away. Far more than the things inside that had caught Tosin's attention. The privilege of being able to witness something so spectacular and the potential to do it every day for the rest of his life was far more valuable to him than the yacht they stood on. Though he had to admit that, as a vehicle for bringing his dreams to life, this one was pretty damn impressive.

Even Miguel seemed to thaw a bit. He ran his fingers over the glossy live-edge tabletops before sinking onto one of the stools arranged around it. It wasn't hard to tell which place was his since his favorite top-shelf liquor was set out, ready and waiting for him.

Tosin's and Archer's, too.

Miguel grabbed the shot of Macallan whiskey and downed it in a single gulp before slamming the glass onto the table with a resounding clunk. He hadn't had time to swallow before a well-dressed crew member appeared, seemingly from nowhere, with a refill.

When the man had disappeared once more, Archer sat too, his fingers picking at the edges of the folder Banks had left there for him. Where the hell did they start?

Miguel helped him out.

"So you fucking lied to us? You're loaded? This whole time, were you looking down your nose at us? Laughing at how pitiful we were?" He crossed his arms, looking toward the exit as if he might dart out of there faster than a rainbow runner, leaving Archer blinking at the vanishing back of his friend.

His worst fears began to come true. He would be rejected, judged undeserving of his companions' respect. Fucked over by his inheritance. If the only thing these two guys could see was his net worth, then no one else in the universe would do differently. They knew him better than anyone else.

Pain stabbed his chest. He rubbed the ache, but it didn't fade.

The worst thing he could imagine was dying as alone as his father had been, accompanied only by bought sycophants.

"Hey, don't be like that." Tosin punched Miguel in the biceps. "He's lived with us for twelve years. Roughing it. Having fun even when we didn't have a lot else. Why don't you let him tell us why? I would like to hear that."

Fair enough. Archer nodded and swallowed hard.

When Miguel faced him again, curiosity in his gaze, Archer confessed, "I hated who I was. The lifestyle, the obligations, and the political maneuvering that left innocent victims in its wake."

He scrunched his eyes closed as a particular face appeared in his mind. Raven hair down to her perfect ass, porcelain skin, and eyes as blue as the spots on the juvenile damselfish he'd stared at not very long ago.

His biggest regret.

The final straw that had sent him packing. "So I opted out of it all. Left. Became someone else entirely."

"You're saying you're not an orphan like you told us forever ago. That's why you never said a peep about home or your family. You're a runaway." Miguel wasn't cutting Archer a lot of slack. The way he sneered *runaway* made it sound sort of like *chicken shit*. Or *quitter*. Two things they definitely didn't respect and never had allowed themselves to be before.

Archer reminded himself that as much of a shock to his system it had been these past few weeks—imagining his life proceeding in an entirely different direction from what he'd planned—for these two, hearing these things would be the equivalent of taking a polar bear plunge into the Arctic after a decade of tropical swims.

They probably had no idea some people really lived like this.

Until you'd seen it yourself, it was impossible to really visualize.

At least that's what he'd been told by Banks.

"It wasn't exactly a lie. My father was dead to me. Or maybe I was reborn. I walked away when I was nineteen and never looked back. My father said he would disown me the instant I crossed his threshold. I thought he had. I didn't care. About a month ago, he kicked the bucket and left me everything. So, now it is true. I *am* the last of my family. Before I'd only wished that was the case."

"How can you say something so cold?" Miguel—who had lost his parents in an accident when he was eight and grown up in a group home in South America—glared at Archer as if he was more disgusting than the sludge that sometimes accumulated in the corners of their dive boat. "I don't know who you are anymore. Maybe I never did."

He stood in a rush, making his stool tilt precariously, then turned toward the door.

Until Tosin asked quietly, "What did your dad do to you to make you hate him? You don't have a temper and I've never known you to hold a grudge."

"He..." Archer cleared his throat and broke eye contact, staring out the window at the desert paradise he'd come to adore so much when the memories threatened to overwhelm him.

Sitting on his couch, not able to hear the knock on the door right away...staggering to the front door to find it was her. *She'd come to him.*

If only he hadn't been so intoxicated, he might have noticed something was wrong.

If he'd been sober—and his father hadn't been meddling in their lives—he might not have made such a grave and horrible mistake.

Despite the fact that his father deserved his rage, Archer hadn't forgiven himself. Not for his failures as a son. And *definitely* not for falling for his father's twisted scheme. He should have realized what was happening. Should have stopped before she got hurt.

"Fuck this. He's never going to be straight with us. I'm out of here." Miguel turned and strode toward the exit.

"Fine. Wait!" Archer couldn't let him leave. Except the truth might make him run instead of walk. "He set me up. Conned me into raping someone."

The words seared his windpipe as though they'd been made of stonefish venom.

There. He'd admitted it out loud for the first time. Ever.

Maybe that was the first step toward acceptance. Forgiveness would be too generous. He'd never grant himself that kind of absolution from his own self-recriminations.

"Say *what*?" Miguel turned around then, his head cocked. His bright eyes, such a contrast to his olive complexion and midnight hair, bored into Archer. "That doesn't even make sense, dude. How can you accidentally rape someone? This isn't even funny anymore. Did I hit my head underwater or something?"

Archer tried to explain. Nothing would come out through his raw throat. It was his turn to slam his drink and relish the fire it lit within him. He deserved the punishment. "He made me a monster. Just like him. A pawn in his power plays. I realized I couldn't stay. What I'd done was bad enough. If I didn't leave, I was going to become just like him someday. If it wasn't too late already."

He planted his elbows on the table then dropped his head into his hands, trying to ward off the revulsion his ex-best-friends would likely feel toward him now. He wouldn't blame them.

"This is getting sicker and more twisted by the second," Miguel snarled. "How can you still be sitting there, Tosin? Let's go."

Their joint friend looked from one guy to the other. Who would he side with?

Archer braced himself for them both to walk out.

"Calm down a second and think, Miguel." Tosin urged the man to wait. "Don't you remember the night we spent in that skanky Mexican jail for brawling?"

That had him pausing. Consciously or not, he edged a couple steps closer. "Yeah, because this moron got us tangled up in some domestic dispute."

"Right. Does a real rapist stand up for a stranger who's fighting off a dude, who clearly is not taking no for an answer, in a bar bathroom? Does he snap and beat the man to a pulp?"

Archer clearly recalled the flash of fury that had overtaken him in that instant.

"Maybe they do if they feel guilty about what they've done," Miguel answered, his voice a lot softer now.

"I do. I regret what happened. Every day. Every hour. The woman I hurt... She's spectacular. Special."

"Why don't you tell us the full story?" Tosin asked.

"I—can't." Archer shook his head. "The details don't matter anyway. They would sound like excuses. I did it. I accept responsibility for it. But I wasn't about to hang around and let anyone put me in those kinds of situations again."

"I'm going to have to disagree on that point. I feel like you owe us the rest." Tosin ruffled Archer's hair briefly before polishing off his own liquor. "Someday soon. A less crazy day than today, tell us. I have a feeling we might see it differently. Seems like you could use a sounding board on this one."

Archer dreaded that conversation, though he knew they'd have to have it.

Wait.

"Does that mean you're planning on sticking around, then?" He could hardly breathe.

Tosin nodded, a faint smile curving his lips. "For over ten years, we've done everything together. Trusted each other. I know you, Archer. You're not the person you obviously think you are. *Right*, Miguel?"

Archer risked a glance at his partner. The guy seemed unsure. With one foot out the door, he studied Archer's face. Hopefully he could read the genuine remorse there. A lifetime of regret wouldn't be enough to change what had happened that night, but he desperately wished it could.

Sometimes even a Scrooge McDuck-sized fortune couldn't buy your way out of a problem.

Some things weren't for sale.

Like forgiveness.

Or a time machine.

Or the faith of your two best friends.

Living with mistakes as awful as Archer's could cost a man his soul.

"Shit!" Miguel ran his hands through his hair, then pivoted. Step by step, he returned. He fell onto the barstool, looking as deflated as Archer felt. "I'm gonna need another drink."

No sooner had he said it than his wish came true.

The three guys glanced between each other, weirded out and enjoying the indulgence simultaneously.

"So basically, you came into a crap ton of money and decided to buy a megayacht and live out the rest of your life in luxury?" Tosin hummed. "Not a bad plan, really."

"That's not exactly what I had in mind." Archer shrugged before opening the folder in front of him. "I had Banks draw up some contracts. I'd like you to read them. It should make everything clear."

Already he sounded like the tool his father had always hoped he'd become. When stakes were this high, he supposed some formalities couldn't be avoided. He handed each of his friends a copy of the agreement he hoped they'd sign.

Tosin skimmed his before asking, "You're offering us a job? All that stuff we were joking around about on the beach. That's what you actually intend to do, isn't it?"

Archer nodded. "Yes. I've appointed Banks to be the executive director of the Banks Foundation. The sole purpose of the organization is to take my money and put it to good use. He asked me a ton of questions about things that are important to me, like women's rights, abuse hotlines, transitional shelters, domestic violence awareness, those kinds of things. But also stuff like conservation, renewable energy sources, and clean drinking water initiatives. He's figuring out how to address as many of those global issues as we can by creating charities dedicated to them and funding research by the world's leading scientists in relevant fields."

"What does that have to do with a megayacht? Is this the headquarters of the Banks Foundation or something?" Miguel asked, sounding truly interested for the first time.

"Not quite." Archer shook his head. "Though Banks will be living onboard and he's the head of the foundation, so...maybe. This is one of the Banks Foundation projects. Banks actually came up with it and talked me into getting personally involved. We're calling it the Divemaster Project, for obvious reasons."

"What exactly is the Divemaster Project supposed to do?" Miguel wondered.

"It'll be just like we talked about earlier. A pretty cushy arm of the Banks Foundation. Deserving passengers will join us for a while at sea. We'll foot the bill and try to tip the karma scales in their favor a little. Reward them for whatever it is they've done to not be assholes like some humans. Banks is taking care of the administrative shit. He'll be sourcing the guests for us. Making all the arrangements for them. Managing the staff. We'd be mostly business as usual with a few extra perks. We'd live here and act as the divemasters on the *Divemaster*."

"So we'd work for you?" Tosin's brows drew together, causing some fine wrinkles to show on his forehead. "Not that I think you'd be a bad boss—"

"No. Stop, please." Archer didn't bother to let him finish. "Nothing changes between us. I want you to be my partners like always."

Miguel, who paid the best attention to detail of the three of them, scanned the paper he'd accepted from Archer. He mumbled, "'...eligible to purchase a one-third share of the *Divemaster* for the price of a single US penny.'"

Tosin's jaw dropped.

Miguel continued, "'With the stipulation that should you decide to terminate your stay onboard permanently, you'll offer your share to the Banks Foundation for full market value before listing it for sale publicly.'"

"Archer, that's nuts." Arms flung wide, Tosin interrupted. "A third of this thing has to be at least—"

"Eighty-five million dollars, give or take. Probably more in a few years." He shrugged. "I know what it's like to be trapped by this lifestyle. That's not what I want for either of you. If there comes a day you're ready to get out, you'll still be able to enjoy the things you'll become accustomed to while staying here. Worst case would be if you hung around longer than you wanted to and came to resent me because of something as unimportant as money. You're free to stay here forever...or go. At any time. I'd never lock you in."

"Can I ask something rude?" Miguel leaned forward. He didn't wait for permission before shooting out his questions. "Just how motherfucking loaded are you? And why does Banks have your name if you're not related?"

Tosin didn't blink as he waited for Archer to respond. He must have been wondering, too.

"Actually, *I've* got *his* name. He was our butler, although that doesn't really convey everything he handled. You know, like raising me and shit. I borrowed it when I went incognito, hiding from my father. Every day, Banks showed me the kind of person I wanted to be like when I got the chance to make myself."

He'd held himself to that standard. Except for violating that girl... He couldn't let himself think of her now, though. That's what nightmares were for.

"I should have realized that conniving bastard knew where I was all along. Anyway, on my birth certificate, my last name is Quartermane."

"Like the software company?"

"Yeah. That's where my father made most of his money. But I sold everything and put it in some kind of trust. Well, actually, Banks did it for me. I tried not to listen when he told me about it. All I care about is that this obscene amount of cash makes a positive impact. I don't want anything else to do with it."

Tosin looked like he'd gulped down a few lungfuls of seawater. "So, what you're saying is...you're a goddamned multi-billionaire?"

"More or less." Archer shrugged. "If it was all sitting in my bank account it'd probably be five, six, maybe seven, billion depending on the day and the stock markets. I don't plan to touch a cent other than what we've got in the yacht and her expenses. Banks assured me the essentials are more than taken care of by the interest on several long-term investments dedicated to the holding company that technically purchased the yacht, which we will also jointly own. Blah blah blah, whatever. Long story short, we can do this. Forever, if you guys don't get sick of it. And if you do, you're welcome to go try whatever else makes you happy instead."

Tosin reached into the pocket of his cargo shorts. He slapped his hand onto the table, leaving a penny on top of Archer's now-empty folder. "Reporting for duty."

Together, Tosin and Archer looked at Miguel.

"I've just got one more question," he sighed.

"What the hell could matter after all that?" Veins popped out in Tosin's neck as he practically had a coronary. "Pull your head out of your ass and sign on the dotted line, fuckface. Do it now, or so help me I will come over there and do it for you."

"Hear him out." Archer put his hand on Tosin's shoulder and pressed steadily yet firmly. "It's okay. What else do you want to know, Miguel?"

"Will you lend me a penny? I spent the last of my cash on that second helping back at the street-meat wagon." For dramatic effect, he paused before adding, "I'm good for it. I swear."

Laughter burst from Archer's chest. It was either that or surrender to the burn behind his eyes. "For real? You're coming, too?"

"You're not going anywhere without me, bro." Miguel held his fist out over the center of their table.

Tosin and Archer took turns bumping it before doing the same to each other.

They stared around, dazed, until Miguel said, "I can't believe that really happened."

"I'm still in shock myself." Though the oily grime finally seemed to be dissipating from Archer's guts some.

Eyes narrowed, Miguel growled, "When, exactly, did your dad pass away?"

"My guess, a month ago." Tosin's features regained some of his storminess. "This is what the fuck has been wrong with you. You've been freaking out. And you didn't say a damn word."

"I think that pisses me off more than you forgetting to mention you were a billionaire." Disappointment cast a shadow on Miguel's acceptance.

"I'm sorry." It felt good for Archer to finally give them the apology they hadn't known they'd deserved before. "I swear, from now on, no more secrets."

Quick to anger, but faster to forgive, Miguel nodded. "So now what the fuck do we do?"

Tosin stood. "Yo, Banks, you out there somewhere?"

A few seconds later, he rejoined them in the bar with a flute of champagne in his hand. "Celebrations are in order, yes?"

"Yes," Archer practically roared with relief.

"To the divemasters." Banks drained his glass as well.

The three guys cheered for him.

"First order of business, I want that tour you promised, Banks." Tosin slapped the older guy on the back, knocking him forward a little.

"I would recommend you boys go quit your jobs first." The guy probably had a schedule etched into his brain. He would keep them organized. Thank God.

Archer would have felt bad about leaving their shop in a lurch with such short notice if Banks hadn't already arranged for a dozen candidates, who would be flown in—or maybe had been already—for their shop manager to interview.

Confirming Archer's suspicions, Banks continued, "If you don't leave now, your replacements might arrive at the shop before you give notice. That could be a kind of awkward, don't you think?"

"The dude seriously thinks of everything, doesn't he?" Miguel stared at Banks in awe.

"It's my job, *sir*."

Miguel squirmed like Archer did when Banks *sir*ed him. Somehow that was way funnier when it was happening to his friend.

"Okay, fine," Tosin amended. "First we quit. Then we get our tour. And after that, I think we should throw one hell of a going away party onboard."

Miguel stiffened.

A wince crossed Tosin's face. "I mean, if that's okay with you, Archer."

"Guys, let's get one thing straight right now." He stared at both of his best friends. "We're in this as equals. You have every right to make decisions. In fact, let's sign those contracts and make it official. The last thing I'd want is for this to fuck up our friendship. Things should be the same..."

"But hella better!" Miguel held out his hand in a silent promise and Archer clasped it. The other guy drew him in for a man-hug, clapping him on his back a few times hard enough to rattle his organs around. "I don't know what to say."

"*I* say, here's to new adventures." Archer swallowed against the lump in his throat as he caught Banks's wink from behind Miguel. They'd done it.

For once, he was starting to believe it might be okay to enjoy this opportunity his father had left him.

"And *I* say...party time, boys!" Tosin jogged down the hall, burst out the door, and shouted loud enough over the rail to the bystanders gathered below that Archer, Miguel, and Banks had no trouble hearing him despite the soundproofing. "Who's ready for a wild time?"

Archer was.

SIX

"**A**rchie! Yo, Arrrrchiiiieeeeee." Shitfaced and amped up, the guys had decided they liked Banks's nickname for him a little too much. It was going to be hell getting them to stop calling him that.

He winced then pitched his voice over the music, which pumped across the deck they were partying on. "Over here, Miguel."

"I brought you a going away present." He tugged a gorgeous woman in an ultra-feminine sarong dress behind him as he cut through the crowd. Long, tan legs peeked from thigh-high gaps in the sides as she walked. A fresh hibiscus adorned the clip holding her wavy hair back from her face. When she looked up, Archer recognized her despite the subtle touches of makeup—something she didn't ordinarily wear— highlighting her already striking features.

The kite-surfing street-meat dealer.

"Hey." For the first time in weeks, his cock perked up at the sight of a very willing woman.

It wasn't permanently broken! Hallelujah!

Mistaking his enormous grin as an invitation, she plastered herself to his side and gave him a hug as big as if she were an octopus wrapping all eight tentacles around him simultaneously. He found himself reflexively returning the gesture. Who was he to squash a woman's hopes?

Sure, he'd promised himself he wouldn't fool around for the hell of it anymore, but tonight had turned out to be one of the best of his life.

He deserved to celebrate. Besides, she'd tried to get with him before she'd known he was rich, so he already preferred her to the dozens of circling sharks who smelled cash in the water.

Bonaire wasn't a very big island. Rumors had spread from one end to the other before he, Tosin, and Miguel had even packed up their cabanas. He swore half the population had crammed themselves onboard tonight, suddenly acting as if they were long-lost relatives.

Archer much preferred the genuine bond he had with his partners, and women like this one.

"Hi." She backed off just far enough to extend her hand. "I'm Savannah. Nice to officially meet you, finally."

"Likewise." He brought her hand to his mouth and kissed her knuckles. Afterward he didn't let go, entwining their fingers instead. "Would you prefer to go somewhere quieter, so we can talk? Or were you looking forward to dancing?"

"Whatever you want."

Ugh. No. There'd be time for that later, once he had her splayed out across his bed. He liked his partners to have a strong will so that when they chose to surrender to him, he knew he'd won something truly precious. Something he'd thought he'd earned from *her.* "Lady's choice."

"Dancing." She smiled up at him, kind of shyly. Yet still seductive, full of promise.

The evening was about to get even better.

"Thanks." He nodded to Miguel as he passed. "I owe you one."

"I think you've covered it already." His friend slapped him on the ass.

They both laughed at that. It didn't feel like he'd done much of anything. With Banks's guidance, he had changed their lives forever, he supposed. Selfishly, Archer had mostly considered that he didn't want to leave his best friends behind when he embarked on the next phase of his life. If that made him an asshole, so be it. In the end, each of them had benefitted.

When they'd made it to the center of the floor, people parting to let him pass, Archer spun Savannah around then swallowed her up with his arms and tugged her close. He let his hips grind against hers, giving her a calculated preview of what the rest of the evening could have in store for them.

It only took a few songs for her to ride his thigh and begin pressing her chest, including her pebbled nipples, into the patch of tan skin his partially opened dress shirt exposed. She stared up at him with a blend of heat and desire that he was not about to waste.

"I think I'd like to see that quieter place now, if you don't mind," she said just loud enough to be heard despite the pulsating beats.

Soon enough she'd shatter the calm of whatever nook he hauled her off to by crying out his name as she came. She'd triggered his instincts with her sweet request, and he was about to exceed her expectations.

Some people might consider him egotistical, but he preferred to think of himself as frank about his skill level as a lover.

Archer excelled at seduction.

With a hand in the small of Savannah's back, he guided her through the throng, angling his shoulders to protect her from being jostled by frenzied revelers.

There was one place he hadn't checked out on the ship yet.

Time to rectify that oversight.

Archer didn't feel like stopping to gawk at the yacht's interior. Instead, he scooped Savannah into his arms and allowed her to think of it as a romantic gesture. Her heartbeat tripped beneath the fingers he curled around her ribs.

Without speaking, she rested her head on his shoulder, and he knew he'd won. She was his for the taking. And he would give all of himself in return. For a little while.

When he reached his destination, he cradled her with one arm, and used a palm scanner to unlock a smoky black glass door. Then he brought Savannah inside, waiting for her telltale gasp.

She didn't disappoint, making his cock twitch in his khaki shorts. "What *is* this place?"

Now *that* was a good question. During their many discussions about the *Divemaster*, Archer had told Banks he thought it would be a good idea to have a place the guys could relax discreetly with any personal guests they might choose to entertain. One that didn't require inviting them to their private space. It seemed the guy had used his imagination and taken things over the top. Maybe Archer's father wasn't the only one who'd kept tabs on him. Could the divemasters' penchant for visiting sex clubs have been notated in some report?

He bet it had been.

Tosin and Miguel were going to lose their minds, or come in their pants, when they realized the extent of the facilities onboard. Looked like the *Divemaster* still had some secrets to uncover. He wasn't surprised—the more they'd explored, the more they realized how huge it was. There hadn't been much time between when they'd gotten back from the dive shop and guests started arriving, either.

"Looks like it's our private playroom."

"I like to play," she purred. Then, without hesitation, she began to strip. First her dress, then her matching lace bra and boy-short panties. When she stood naked before him, she sank to her knees, reaching for the waistband of his shorts.

Just like *she* had, making him feel like she craved him as he had her.

Too bad he could have been anyone with a cock, and she would have reacted the same way.

Archer shook his head and concentrated on Savannah.

She wasn't subtle or tentative as she unbuttoned then unzipped his shorts. That was fine with him. He didn't need her to be.

Archer whipped his shirt over his head and dropped it beside her clothes. Then he shoved his shorts and briefs to the ground, stepping out of them. Since he was already barefoot, there weren't any shoes to deal with. Handy.

When Savannah licked her lips, staring at his erection, he shot her a wicked grin.

Archer grasped her face between his palms and held her in place while he bent down to steal a kiss. She moaned and responded, opening to his demanding tongue.

After he'd taken his fill, he speared his fingers into her hair and directed her to his aching balls. She licked them, in no way hesitant as she nuzzled his groin, sucking gently while she bathed them with the flat of her tongue.

"Yes, that's it." He encouraged her like a teacher with a student. There wasn't anything tender about it. That's not what either of them was here for. "Just for that amazing job you're doing down there, I promise to give you plenty of orgasms before the night is through."

It seemed she appreciated his dirty talk as much as most women did.

Would *she* have? He hadn't tried it since he'd only had affectionate things to say to *her*.

Savannah redoubled her efforts, lavishing her attention on his cock as well.

He didn't bother to hide how well she played his body. Instead, when she took him to the back of her throat, he rewarded her enthusiastic sucking by limiting the time she needed to spend on her knees.

Archer tugged her hair, pinning her close to his abdomen, then came down her throat in a rush complete with a series of heartfelt groans. She swallowed around him eagerly, drawing out his pleasure.

When he withdrew, leaving a sheen on her lush lips, he reached down and lifted her to her feet.

"Thank you," he rasped before sealing his mouth over hers and making sure she knew he meant it. Savannah might not be *her*, but he appreciated her generosity in sharing herself nonetheless. Damn, he'd needed that fast, hard release to take the edge off.

Now there'd be plenty of time to recover before demonstrating he had better stamina than a horny teenager. Though he'd done well—too well—with *her*.

They'd screwed for hours before he realized what was going on.

Savannah reminded him to stay in the present. The party below decks was just getting started.

"You're welcome." She smiled up at him, glancing around the floor as if preparing to make a grab for her dress.

"Oh, hell no." He stopped her with his curt command. "That's not how I roll. Get your sexy ass over to that…whatever the fuck that thing is."

Archer pointed at a contraption that seemed like the world's craziest dentist chair. Black leather, straps everywhere, segmented and fully adjustable seat sections. Oh yeah, that would do.

If he wasn't mistaken, she whimpered then shivered before practically dashing to the equipment.

"That's better," he growled as he stalked to her, arranging her to suit his intentions before buckling her in for one hell of a wild ride.

Archer crouched between her spread thighs, feasting on her for so long his mind blissed out and all his worries faded away. Including the ones about how disastrously this could end up in the morning.

No matter how bad it was, it couldn't possibly be his worst morning after.

Trying to shove those thoughts away, he applied himself to maximizing Savannah's pleasure as if it was some kind of penance. He'd stopped counting the number of climaxes he gave her as he steadily jerked himself back to full hardness. By the time she went limp, her thighs quivering against his shoulders, he was ready to fuck.

It was right about then that the door opened.

Archer rose, blocking as much of his partner from prying eyes as he could.

He shouldn't have worried. It was only Miguel with a lady, or three, of his own. Kind of hard to count precisely since his entourage merged with Tosin's, who followed right behind.

The space was big enough for them to keep out of each other's way. Or not, if that's how they rolled. He didn't give a shit if they saw him plowing into Savannah's pretty pussy, as he planned to do in a just a few more seconds. But how would she feel about it?

"I need to be fucked, Archer. Let them watch what you do to me." She surprised him with her steady plea. "I don't care about anything except having your cock in me. Now."

He couldn't agree more. Like diving, fucking was one of the few things that could turn off his obsession with the past. It was hard not to compare every partner to *her*, but he tried. It wasn't fair. They would never measure up to perfection. Or at least what he'd thought was total compatibility.

Though he heard his two best friends cheering on the action as they got into some fun of their own, Archer's attention didn't drift from his temporary partner unless it was because of rogue thoughts. Of *her*. Always *her*.

Plucking a condom from a bowl on a table nearby, he tore open the package and sheathed himself. Without torturing either of them longer than he already had, he set the tip of his cock at the opening to Savannah's pussy and bored inside.

The slick channel, prepped by his feasting, admitted him easily.

At least when coaxed by his unrelenting forward pressure.

He let his head drop back so he could savor the fisting of her flesh around his. Once he bottomed out, he began to retreat.

Archer took it slow until they'd both adjusted to the sensations, then began to drill into Savannah with a steady and fluid motion that shattered her around him a couple of times within the first few minutes. The squeeze and ripple of her muscles against his cock was enough to have him gritting his teeth while he rubbed light circles around her clit, keeping her aroused.

Still not as tight as *she* had been. Virginal, until he'd ruined her.

As he really dug in, he leaned forward. The graceful arch of Savannah's neck tempted the animal within him. He wrapped his fingers around it lightly, careful not to come close to hurting her. It might make him a savage, but there was no denying he loved this feeling.

Being in control.

Granting them both pleasure by revealing his inner beast.

It might make him hate himself later. Confuse the hell out of him. But he'd worry about that some other time.

One of his friends' companions edged nearer for a close-up view of the action. Archer fucked harder, faster, fulfilling each of Savannah's moaned pleas, which encouraged him to intensify their experience.

And when she seemed to stall, on the very edge of one final epic release, the female bystander graciously helped him out. He hoped Miguel or Tosin would treat her especially well for her generosity.

Because when she leaned in and captured Savannah's mouth in a gentle kiss he would have been utterly incapable of bestowing to anyone but *her*, she shuddered and clenched on his shaft, threatening to fracture his cock.

Archer roared then poured jet after jet of come into the condom he wore.

He half expected to see that he'd ripped a hole in it with the force of the blasts when he withdrew from Savannah's still-twitching pussy. Thankfully, he hadn't.

Dripping sweat and high on endorphins, he released her as quickly as possible, rubbing her wrists and ankles to return full circulation.

The entire time, she made out with their new arrival. It should have been every man's fantasy come to life. Except now that he was utterly spent, fucked dry, Archer found himself wishing he hadn't done it at all.

It had only reminded him that no one could replace *her*. Was he doomed to be unsatisfied with even fantastic sex for the rest of his life? It would serve him right, he supposed.

The only problem was he'd utterly exhausted this free-spirited woman, and he refused to walk away and leave her in such a vulnerable state. Even though he knew Miguel and Tosin would tend to her properly, it wasn't their responsibility.

For tonight only, it was his.

And he'd sworn he would never let another woman down. Like he had *her*.

The guys had obviously been inspired by his show. They didn't bother to say goodnight when he gathered Savannah to his chest and passed by them as the group of ladies spoiled his friends rotten. Good for them all, if that's what made them happy.

Archer ignored his better judgment and took Savannah to his room, both of them completely naked. If he encouraged her to stay over, maybe he could pretend that what they'd shared meant more than simple physical relief.

It didn't work.

He should have been sated. Instead, he felt hollow.

And she...well, she was knocked out by the time he'd made it down the hall.

All through the night, Archer kept Savannah close, watching over her. No matter what, he appreciated the raw passion she'd shared with him and did his best to meet her needs beyond sticking his dick in her.

As if he might float away or cease to exist if he let his eyes close, he blinked up at the night sky visible through the domed glass ceiling.

Despite everything around him, or maybe because of it, he felt insignificant. Incomplete.

His eyelids never drooped. Propped against pillows and the headboard, he ran his fingers through Savannah's hair, happy to give her what she craved for the few hours they had left together. Wishing someone other than *she* could do that for him. Even while dreaming, she curled closer to his touch.

Maybe someday he'd find another person who could inspire that kind of reaction in him. He'd be the richest man in the universe if, when he did, the woman capable of taming him felt the same in return.

He would do anything to deserve her love. Because all the money in the world couldn't keep him from drowning in loneliness, which made it impossible to sleep.

Hours later, early morning sunlight gilded Archer's cabin, which was a grossly understated label for these quarters. He'd have to figure out where the controls for the automatic blinds were before he actually attempted to sleep in here. It was dazzling, and kind of blinding, to watch the sunrise from his new home. The entire ceiling of his suite was constructed of aqua-tinted glass. It was almost as if he had camped outside.

If camping meant sleeping on a cloud in climate-controlled air while staring at the stars.

Though he knew they were on a boat, the size of the ship and the insignificance of the chop in Bonaire's sheltered port had made it as steady as a rock. He couldn't possibly have been more comfortable.

Unless he'd shared his bed with someone he cared for.

Idiot. From now on, he would stick to his plan.

Savannah began to rouse beside him, stretching and yawning into her fist. She was beautiful mussed, but he immediately began to think of ways to avoid a round of morning sex he simply wasn't into. It wouldn't be fair to mislead her.

Banks to the rescue again.

A non-intrusive tone chimed from beside the bed. It was subtle enough that Archer didn't register it as an incoming phone call until the third ring. He reached over to the side table to answer. "Yes?"

"Morning, Archie. Our final crew member is onboard. When you and the other divemasters are recovered from last night, I'd like to hold a staff meeting. We should get introductions out of the way and talk about some ground rules before the first set of guests begin arriving this afternoon. Does that work for you?"

"Of course, I'll be right out." Truthfully, he couldn't be more glad that Banks had spared him an awkward goodbye. "I'll stop and get the guys on my way. Otherwise, they'll never make it."

"Probably wise. They seemed to be enjoying themselves last night." Banks pitched his voice lower. "I left Ms. Ridley's garments outside your door and there's a breakfast buffet waiting. You're welcome."

Then he hung up.

Archer rolled out of bed and collected their belongings. He left them on the bed while he used the restroom and yanked on some clothes. When he returned, Savannah shimmied into her discarded dress. She hadn't made any demands, for which he was grateful. Still, he felt familiar disappointment tainting the pleasure they'd brought each other the night before.

If he'd felt something for her—even a faint echo of the something he'd felt for his long-ago girl—he could have justified bringing Savannah along on their journey. Unfortunately, their sexual chemistry seemed to be the extent of their connection. Just like it had been with all the women he'd enjoyed.

Except one.

The one he couldn't have.

The one he'd caused irreparable harm.

Archer opened the door and Savannah stepped into the hallway. She smiled up at him.

"I hope you'll stop by for lunch again someday...when you're good and *hungry*." The way she practically purred the last part made it clear what kind of appetite she hoped to slake.

He might have made an empty promise then, if he hadn't seen a ghost out of the corner of his eye. Had he summoned it by thinking about *her*?

What the—?

A uniformed crew member darted past, head down, as if embarrassed to have interrupted his obvious morning-after farewell. It must have been a trick of the light, or maybe his guilty conscience for breaking his promise to keep his dick in his pants until he'd made a meaningful match with someone, because he could have sworn it was *her.*

Or someone who looked like she might now—grown, gorgeous, strong.

He was going to have to find out who that actually was so he could stay far, far away.

Fortunately, he was about to enter a staff meeting and learn her name. Some part of him couldn't deny the morning's job requirements had just gotten a lot less onerous.

"Let me walk you out," he said to Savannah.

She smiled wistfully, then shook her head. "No need. Thanks for an unforgettable evening. I'm glad we got a chance to do that before you left. It was everything I hoped it would be."

Archer kissed her cheek. He wished he could feel more for her than he did.

Without looking back, Savannah swayed down the hall, off the boat, and out of his life.

He couldn't do this again. He swore he was going to hold out for someone who meant something to him. Someone he couldn't live without. Otherwise, disappointment might crush him.

It hurt too much to think he was the kind of man who found it this easy to turn away affection.

What kind of coldhearted bastard did that make him?

One just like his father.

Fuck.

Lieutenant Commander Waverly Adams squared her shoulders, assuming her military-grade posture. She strode down the hall from her assigned bunk, where she'd dropped off her midnight blue camo duffle. It was hard to believe that as part of the crew she had a room, however cramped, to herself. Hell, it even had a porthole to let in natural light and give her a glimpse of paradise outside the ship.

After a dozen years of living in barracks, she would so take that.

If she stayed.

Waverly headed toward the stairs that led to the upper deck, where their staff meeting would be held. Her heart pounded in her chest. It felt odd to have her hair down, brushing her butt. Even braided, it seemed wild compared to twisting, wrapping, and pinning her mane into a bun that conformed to the Navy's strict grooming standards.

Something had urged her to shed a couple of those uptight habits. Maybe so her old acquaintance would have some hint of the kid she'd been to jog his memory.

Would Archer Quartermane—her first and everlasting crush—even remember her?

She thought so, but feared that he might not.

What if, like so many other people who'd faded from her life, he'd meant much more to her than she had to him? Sure, they'd gone to different schools. Hers a private, all-girls preparatory academy. His even more exclusive. But he'd hung out with her sporadically for years at pretty much every event they'd found each other at, when both of their fathers had been required to attend.

It had gotten to the point where the first thing she'd do when she could break away from shaking hands and looking pretty by her father's side was beg the doorman to check the guest list for Archer's father. Even the most boring events had been tolerable when he had been there to help her pass the time.

As they got older, their haphazard run-ins had turned into flirt fests.

One evening in particular had occupied a disproportionate amount of her teenaged daydreams. They'd been out exploring a hedge maze on the grounds of some socialite's mansion, laughing and chasing each other around the fountain at the center, when she'd tripped on her gown and crashed into him.

To keep her from bashing her brains out on a cherub statue, which pissed into the basin—how the fuck was that supposed to be classy anyway?—he'd caught her against his chest. It had started making the transition from scrawny to the broad torso of a grown man. His sheer size, the flex of his muscles, and his general...hardness...had amazed her. He must have liked what he'd felt, too. Because, as he steadied her on her feet, he leaned in.

Waverly had held her breath, afraid to hope that she might share her first kiss ever with Archer.

He'd made her unspoken wish come true.

The rest of that summer they'd skipped the chasing and gone straight to making out whenever they could find a shadowy corner, an abandoned boathouse, or an intricate garden.

Even now, the memory of his lips on hers and the remembered comfort his protective arms around her had the power to make her swoon. The warrior in her hated to admit it since the woman she'd grown into was nothing like the naïve, entitled brat she'd been before he'd taken off without warning—right around the time her fairy tale upbringing had officially gone to shit.

Waverly figured she'd had to crash and burn to truly appreciate life.

After all, starting over from scratch had allowed her to rebuild herself from the ground up, into the fierce, independent, competent person she was proud to be today. According to Banks, that would be another thing she had in common with her new boss. Something sure to earn his respect.

It had been a long time since she'd felt this vulnerable or sought someone's approval.

This was either the best or worst idea she'd ever had.

They were about to find out which it was.

Lost in thought, she jogged up the staff staircase that dumped out into the main hallway two floors above. She hadn't gone more than ten paces when the door immediately in front of her opened. Out stepped

Archer along with a lovely—if rumpled—woman who'd clearly spent the night in his bed.

Whoa.

Waverly hadn't prepared herself for the pang of jealousy that threatened to unsheathe her formidable claws. Worse, attraction flared inside her as she caught a whiff of Archer's clean, masculine scent along with a peek at his melted-chocolate eyes.

Gorgeous and untouchable as ever.

She ducked her head and practically dashed along the immaculate hardwood past the couple. Her bare feet slapped some as she hustled in the direction of the lounge where Banks had instructed her to join their upcoming gathering.

When she turned the corner, she paused to regain her balance, safely out of sight.

It wasn't the ship tilting. It was her.

As if it wasn't weird enough being here—in circumstances so different than all those years before yet no less awkward—coming face-to-face with Archer and his latest lover didn't do much for her attempts to loosen up. Especially when a fraction of a second in his presence made it clear he was out of her league in every way that mattered.

Rich. Yup.

Suave. Yup.

Handsome. Yup.

A lover, not a fighter. Yup.

Capable of enjoying a casual hookup. Yup.

Archer had exactly zero things in common with the safe, boring men she accepted dinner invitations from on occasion.

Waverly drew in a deep breath, concentrating on settling down. She'd need to rely on her training to get her job here done despite being in constant close quarters with the only man who'd ever made her systems go haywire. And apparently still did.

It had been years since she'd wrestled with her confidence like this. That could be why she had come. It required proving to herself that she could handle things now that had been insurmountable obstacles before. A new challenge.

Except she might have gotten in over her head. The onslaught of memories, none of them as precious as the ones Archer had made with her, threatened to suffocate her. It had all been downhill from there. She just hadn't known it yet.

Cool, controlled, and skilled, she'd flown rescue missions the military wouldn't entrust to anyone else. Why did it feel like this time she might be the one who needed some saving?

Waverly stared at her hot pink pedicure. A bold, feminine display since she traipsed around barefoot. In the Navy, she had kept her girly selections hidden in her boots. Another dirty little secret. She should have realized that everything about this job would be different than what she'd grown used to. The drastic shift—not to mention the rekindling of her inappropriate attraction—left her raw and exposed.

On the *Divemaster*, there was nowhere to hide.

"Everything all right?" Banks asked, startling her.

She snapped to attention. "Yes, sir."

"It seems we're both going to have to work on cutting that out." The butler turned executive-agent-of-Archer's-life slung an arm around her shoulder. Grateful for his warmth and support, she leaned into the affectionate gesture just a bit. "Archie gets cranky if you *sir* him."

"Good to know." She definitely didn't want to piss him off.

Banks tugged on her braid. "And I am a simple servant. I don't deserve the title."

She slapped his gut with the back of her hand, making him *oomph*. "Bullshit."

"See, you're much tougher than I am." He murmured, "Stronger than you think, I bet."

If Waverly hadn't sworn off crying for good, she might have been tempted to give in to the sting behind her eyes right then. "Thank you."

"Anytime." He gave her one last squeeze then released her. "Come on. Let's feed you some breakfast and introduce you to the rest of the crew."

She nodded, afraid of what her voice might sound like if she attempted to speak.

Within the lounge, she discovered a situation that was at least sort of familiar. A group of high-performing individuals gathered around bulk-prepped food, exchanging banter before things got serious. When she entered, many surreptitious yet appraising glances were aimed in her direction.

Nothing new there.

Their combined scrutiny didn't impact her like the thought of a single glance from Archer did.

She hadn't even made it all the way into the room when a man—slightly less than six feet tall, she guessed—set down his plate and made his way to her. He had brown hair dark enough that she might have thought it was black if the sun hadn't shone through the windows onto it. Of course, it was also peppered with some gray that gave him a distinguished air. Gray eyes evaluated her from behind squared-off glasses that were both somewhat nerdy and very flattering. His goatee and mustache, an indulgence he wouldn't have been permitted in the military, were close-cropped and neat. The unmistakable black stripe adorned with an anchor above four gold stripes made it perfectly clear who he was even before Banks completed pleasantries.

"Captain Alex, I'd like you to meet Lieutenant Commander Waverly Adams."

She returned his firm handshake. "Nice to meet you, sir."

He didn't object to her formality. Banks had filled her in earlier so she knew he was a fellow veteran. No amount of cajoling would convince her to treat him differently.

"I'm glad to have you onboard. You came highly recommended by an old friend of mine—Commander Smith."

As soon as he mentioned one of her mentors, they were off exchanging stories. She had no idea how long they'd stood there while Archer probably finished saying goodbye to his overnight guest, or untangled the other two divemasters—the only other missing staff members—from similar situations.

Long enough for her to polish off a ham, egg, and cheese croissant and forget about her nerves, though. She was chuckling at some antics Captain Alex related when everyone else went quiet.

Her laughter rang out in the silence, drawing the attention of her new bosses.

Waverly froze.

So did Archer.

Their gazes locked. She wondered for a moment if he might actually be Superman with a laser-beam stare. It nearly set her blood boiling.

Until the two guys dragging ass behind him crashed into his back, shoving him forward and severing their link.

She figured it was best to act as if she were on the first day of any normal job. One where she hadn't repeatedly sucked face with the boss in another lifetime or fantasized about him far more often than was healthy ever since.

Waverly straightened her spine, assumed her best resting bitch face, and tucked herself into the corner of the room, behind a few other crew members. That seemed to work.

Archer glanced away to address the room in general. "I apologize for making you wait. Tosin isn't exactly a morning person."

The sleepy—and sort of hung-over—looking guy rolled his eyes, drawing an exasperated sigh from one of his partners. Clearly they were also best friends. They could practically finish each others' sentences.

"Oh, I'm a *hell* of a morning guy. As I was about to demonstrate..."

Banks stepped in before they could deteriorate too much of the professional atmosphere he'd created for the staff. At least not on the very first day of the Divemaster Project. "Okay, everyone, today is show time. Our first batch of guests will arrive in just a few hours. The two dozen passengers have one thing in common. They are all family members of children who passed away unexpectedly. They chose to donate their loved ones' organs and saved countless lives despite their own personal losses. Each person was nominated by the family of a transplant recipient who felt they deserved the vacation of a lifetime. For many of these people, significant stress is a constant part of their daily existence. I see it as our mission to help them forget their personal tragedies for a little while. Or if we can't do that, at least give them some space to reflect in peace and quiet away from their obligations."

Well, that sobered things up real quick.

Damn.

For the first time, Waverly realized another massive benefit of this position. It was one she'd loved about her time as a sailor as well. She'd be doing something to enrich people's lives. Maybe make a small difference, like she wished someone had done for her in her time of need.

With that in mind, she swore to iron out any lingering weirdness with Archer and do the best she could for the beneficiaries of his organization. It would help if he didn't keep ogling her, though.

When she caught him doing it again, he looked away.

Yet every few seconds he repeated the performance.

Was he trying to figure out who she was? Or was he hoping she'd take a hint and leave? Maybe he didn't want to remember where they'd come from any more than she did.

One thing was for sure—he wasn't leveling any smoldering, seductive stares in her direction. Intense, yes. Googly eyes, not so much.

Too bad. That might have been the *only* thing she missed about her old life.

Banks continued his briefing. "We've arranged vacation time and everything imaginable so that this group of guests can stay with us for the next three weeks. During that time we'll visit each of the ABC islands, starting here with Bonaire, then moving to Curaçao and on to Aruba before venturing farther out to sea. There is a chain of uninhabited islands Archer, Tosin, and Miguel have visited briefly in the past that they'd like to explore. Depending on how that goes, we could also make a side trip over to Venezuela. We'll adjust the schedule as needed to accommodate weather or other situations that arise. If there are no questions, I'd like to go around the room and have each of you tell us what you do here, your name, and anything else you'd like to share with our newcomers."

The majority of the crew had worked on this ship for weeks as everything was prepared for their inaugural run. Nearly everyone had experience doing the same work on other vessels before that, each experts in their duties. The *Divemaster* hadn't had a helicopter before the renovations, so Waverly was one of the handful of newbies here today. A masseuse, Vanessa, had introduced herself earlier and stood nearby, along with Maria, an addition to the kitchen staff.

This was the first time the rest of the crew was meeting Archer, Tosin, and Miguel as well. That sort of took precedence, deflecting a lot of the pressure from her.

Waverly listened attentively, though she could feel the blast of Archer's stare from time to time. She ignored him, or tried desperately to, memorizing the names and roles of each person on the team.

Staff was organized into a few main groups—officers, deck crew, engineering, and interior. She didn't really fit anywhere. Along with the ship's medic, massage therapist, and of course the divemasters, Waverly was lumped in with the other specialists. Since she'd been the last to arrive and was standing near the end of the line, she was the final person to run through her spiel.

"Good morning, everyone. I'm the ship's helicopter pilot. I spent the last eleven years training with and flying Seahawks for the Navy." If she wasn't mistaken, Archer seemed to relax visibly as she spoke, so she tossed in a joke. "I promise I won't fly like I have on some of my missions. Easy does it. Unless you ask for a wild ride."

She risked a peek at Archer then, only to find his nostrils flaring.

What had she said…?

Oh, oops, she hadn't meant it like *that*. Shit.

She would have tried to smooth over her gaffe if Tosin Ellis hadn't shot his hand in the air, his eyes growing huge. He shouldn't have bothered since he spoke before anyone could give him permission. "Hold up a second. If she's a super sexy, badass helicopter pilot…does that mean we have a helicopter for her to pilot?"

"Yes, sir." Banks nodded solemnly as a few other staff members attempted to disguise their snorts behind napkins.

"Hells yeah! I call first ride in the chopper, suckers!" Miguel fist pumped as he looked between Tosin and Archer.

The guys laughed along with their counterpart, but choked when Banks interjected, "Seems only fair then that Tosin and Archie take the maiden voyage in the supercars we have on board for shore excursions. I assume a Lamborghini and a Bentley will suffice?"

"Are you shitting us right now?" Miguel clasped his chest over his heart. "You wouldn't joke about something like that, would you?"

"I shit you not, sir," Banks replied with the perfect dose of feigned snootiness.

Waverly tried not to let a smile crack her stolid mask. It was impossible. They were so fun to be around. She felt herself wanting to belong already. A dangerous proposition.

Archer shushed Miguel as best he could. Then he nearly melted her insides when he turned his full attention directly on her. "Sorry, with this dumbass losing his mind over here, I didn't catch your name."

So he didn't recognize her after all.

Her smile dulled, becoming forced.

Banks nodded at her, so she drew herself up and led with the bit she was most proud of even if technically she was retired. "I'm Lieutenant Commander Waverly Adams."

Archer gripped his mouth then wiped his hand down his chin. The motion didn't disguise the fact that his jaw had dropped. Flabbergasted, he practically gasped, "Holy fucking shit. It *is* you."

Not in a *Well, how about that! My long lost puppy love. What the hell have you been up to this past decade? So great to see you again!* sort of way, either.

Color leached from his face. His mouth opened and closed a few times. Then color rushed back into his cheeks. This time it was an unhealthy shade of lava red instead of tan, though.

"Banks. I need to see you out in the hall. Immediately." He marched off without another glance—steamy, intense, or otherwise—in her direction.

So...that hadn't gone well.

Of course not. Since she'd just decided she hoped to stick around.

With everyone gawking at her in utter disbelief, she didn't know what to say.

Or what to do.

After a couple tense minutes and muffled shouts, she had had enough.

"If I don't come back, send a search party, would you please, sir?" she asked Captain Alex.

"I'm more worried about that idiot," she thought she heard the man mutter as she stormed out the door, simultaneously humiliated and crushed.

And pissed off because of it.

⤳ EIGHT ⤲

Archer pivoted, swinging around to face Banks, trying not to bellow.

He failed miserably. "Why the *hell* is she here?"

"Because the lieutenant commander is highly qualified for the position. Overly so, in fact. I only hired the best for you, Archie." Placid expression in place, Banks merely stared back, hands folded in front of his uniform. His ensemble consisted of khaki shorts and a navy polo instead of the full tux required by Archer's asshole father. Somehow the cotton had been pressed and was perfectly crisp.

He clearly took this role no less seriously than he had his estate manager duties.

It was also painfully obvious that he'd endured far worse temper tantrums from Archer's father. Though Banks didn't flinch in the face of Archer's ire—and, to be honest, pure terror—he did seem surprised by the uncharacteristic outburst.

Shit. This wasn't the kind of guy Archer aimed to be. But…*Waverly!*

Seeing her had just about knocked him on his ass. Thinking about her sharing opulent, yet still limited quarters with him…

No. That wouldn't work.

Because one look at her had him forgetting the promises he'd made to himself the night before. As she always had, she turned him on in a heartbeat. It must be some crazy compatible pheromone thing they had going between them. What else could explain this instant and insatiable lust?

It was even more inappropriate now than it had been back then.

When he was sixteen, he'd thought his guaranteed boner in her presence was…well, due to being sixteen and horny every minute of the day. When he was nineteen, he'd thought it was because she might be *the one* for him.

Though they'd never gotten a chance to find out before that possibility had been ruined.

Now that he was thirty-one, he had matured enough to be positive his attraction was driven by something a hell of a lot more potent. And more treacherous. Addictive, too.

Even now, like some creeper, he wished he could spy on her in the other room. See the thick braid of onyx hair that would make the perfect tether as he mounted her from behind and rode…

Damn it.

No!

Not after what he'd done to her. She'd *never* be down for that. And he did not blame her.

Disgusted with himself, he hung his head and tried to think.

Why would she sign on to the *Divemaster*?

Wasn't seeing him as painful for her as seeing her was for him?

And...seriously? She was a kickass helicopter pilot?

Confusion battered him from a dozen directions at once. What the hell was going on here?

He'd never have assumed she'd have to work at all, let alone conquer something as daring and non-traditional as that. If he'd ranked every single job in the world he thought Waverly Adams might have in her lifetime, helicopter pilot would likely have fallen below fire breather in a traveling circus or rattlesnake venom milker or pet food taste-tester.

Had he been responsible for the complete annihilation of the playful, fuzzy bunny she'd been before *that* night?

If so, did it make him even sicker that this ferocious version of her turned him on even more than the softer side had?

How had she convinced her ultra-conservative, elitist father to allow her to enlist in the military?

She was obviously stronger willed than he'd given her credit for.

Add another black mark to his record with her.

Uncounted questions swirled around his brain, paralyzing him.

"If you'd like me to release her and find someone else, I will." Banks tipped his head almost imperceptibly. For him, that was as blatant a dissent as if he'd screamed. "I assure you, though, this wasn't some nepotistic hire. She's ranked at the top of her field. Has several commendations in her file. Besides, Archie, I remember how well you two used to get along. You asked me to keep an eye on her when you left. So I thought—"

"You couldn't have known. But you thought wrong. Get her out of here. Please." For the first time, Archer wished he'd done as Banks had requested and reviewed the staff applications. He'd have crumpled Waverly's and thrown it in the trash.

Or maybe even burned that fucker.

Anything to keep her safe from him.

Because even now, he didn't want her to go.

What kind of insanity was this?

"Excuse me?" Anything but contrite, Waverly stood a few feet away, her brows arched, her hands on her lush hips and her toes tapping against the teak.

Even pissed, she looked amazing.

Pure temptation.

Archer could hardly catch his breath, never mind think straight. Had she come here to demand an apology? If so, he would gladly grovel. It was just that he didn't think acts of contrition would suffice. Words couldn't take back what he'd done.

Or did she plan to haunt him?

His mind scrambled, trying to analyze the problem from every angle, starting with her perspective. The one that mattered most.

What if this wasn't about him at all?

So far she hadn't made it seem as if it was. Hell, she hadn't even mentioned his sins when she could have outed him to a roomful of people.

If that was true, and she was here to prove something to herself, then he owed her anything she desired. If this position was it, he'd have to find a way to bury his attraction to her. Demonstrate that he had preserved some shred of a gentleman in him somewhere, despite his inherited evil streak.

Except he wasn't sure he had.

Even now, he was finding it hard to pry his attention off her breasts and the way they filled out the Banks Foundation shirt she wore. Some part of him roared in satisfaction, seeing his name on her body.

Could putting up with his lechery really be worth it to her?

"Why the hell do you want this job?" he barked at her.

She didn't retreat despite the things she knew he was capable of. The military had hardened her.

Or maybe he had.

"Because I've earned a cushy gig after risking my life for my country this past decade?" She didn't sound a hundred percent convincing when she said it, but he was willing to let it slide.

"Just tell me one thing." He stared at her fingers as he asked. He'd seen her rubbing the hem of her polo between her thumb and forefinger earlier. Right when she'd revealed herself. A classic Waverly tell. He'd know if she lied.

"What?"

"Are you doing this only for the money?" He swallowed hard, downing some of his pride to make as many amends as he could. "You know I'd have Banks write a check right now from the Foundation with as many zeroes as you tell him to add if that's what you're after. It's yours. Anything you need. Or hell, even if it's just what you want from me. No reason to make us both suffer."

The only thing her fingers did was curl into a fist at that last bit. He was liable to end this conversation with a well-deserved shiner if he wasn't careful.

"I think you've lost your mind. Yeah, I took a job for money. That's how most people do things. But...that stuff, about the kids. That means more. I would have liked to have been part of something generous, compassionate, and consequential. Whatever's happening here, though, it's not worth it. You know what? Fuck this. And fuck you." She turned as if to leave.

Archer reached out without thinking. His fingers wrapped around her upper arm to stop her. To turn her to face him. Something.

No matter what his intentions were, they were asinine.

He would have to learn to suppress his instincts around her if she stayed.

He had no right to touch her. Ever again.

So why did electricity arc between them when he did? And why didn't she shrink from the contact?

Archer could no longer figure out if he wanted her to stay—or wanted her to go.

Then he realized he was screwing up again. If she was okay with this, who was he to punish her further by denying her a pretty damn sweet job?

He owed her.

If this was what she called her debt in for, he would make it happen, even if it meant he would be driven insane with remorse and guilt before their first tour was complete. It wouldn't come close to paying for what he'd done.

At least she didn't seem afraid of him. If she had shrunk away, or whimpered, it would have killed him.

Hopefully he could convince her that he would never hurt her again.

Never would have the first time either, if he'd realized what was happening.

Not that it was any excuse.

He was a man now. One intent on doing the right thing, no matter how hard the universe seemed to try making that for him.

"Take your hand off me," she snarled.

Why was he still holding on to her? Part of him was scared she'd storm away and he'd never have the chance to set things to rights. This could be his shot at redemption.

Archer released her. His fingers splayed, palms perpendicular to the floor as he backed away step by step. "I'm sorry, Waverly. It won't happen again."

He hoped she realized he was talking about more than that single stolen touch.

She dusted herself off as if he'd given her cooties then stood straight, defiant, and committed.

Banks stepped between them then, breaking their line of sight and whatever insanity seemed to have overtaken them both. "I have to admit, I've got no idea what's going on here."

"That makes two of us." Waverly threw her hands up.

"Three," Archer growled.

"So why don't we try this? The guests will be here shortly. Call a truce. Go to separate corners of the ship for a while. Tomorrow you can hash things out like adults." The steady calm with which Banks outlined his plan had Archer unwinding slightly. Enough to see the wisdom in his suggestions. "If either of you decide then that I've royally screwed something up, there will be plenty of flights back to the States from Curaçao. For Waverly, or me, or both."

"No one's getting fired." Archer wanted to bang his head on the wall. "But if you want out, either of you…"

"I never intended to upset you. Or Waverly. But I clearly have stepped in it this time." Banks frowned. "There should be repercussions for poor judgment."

"I couldn't agree more," Archer said, thinking this might be payback for his own errors.

Anything he added would take them right back into their argument.

So they left it at that.

For now.

~ NINE ~

Waverly slid her dark sunglasses into place as she wound her way to the bottom level of the yacht and into the divemasters' realm. Not only because it was as if someone had taken the sunlight from Charleston, where she'd been stationed the past eighteen months, and cranked it up about a hundred notches. But also because she needed shielding from Archer's piercing gaze, if yesterday was any indication.

It was sort of like barging into some sea monster's lair. She was determined to plow ahead, though. Shrinking from her fears was not something she believed in doing anymore.

Her fingers trailed along the curved chrome handrail as she descended the final gorgeous staircase that led to the enormous staging area and dive platform. Though she'd never been on a boat this size intended solely for recreation, she was fairly certain these facilities were over the top and custom designed.

Wet suit racks and lockers lined the back wall near the entrance to the interior of the ship. Benches with tank holders and individually assigned milk crate bins tucked beneath each place to keep everyone organized. In the center of the wide-open area, a high counter held camera equipment. There were even a couple of tables being used as desks next to a whiteboard. Tosin appeared to be teaching a handful of guests, who either weren't already certified or were maybe taking an advanced course toward earning a specialty.

Miguel was over by the compressors, refilling tanks. They must have taken a group out far too early for her this morning. Sleeping in was a rare treat. So she'd indulged. Who knew what today would bring? Might as well make the most of what time she had here.

Waverly kept searching, only one person on her mind at the moment.

When she spotted him, bending over in a damn near scandalous pair of white swim briefs that revealed almost all of his fine form, she was even gladder for her cover. Daaaaaaamn!

On display, his ass looked entirely too grab-able. Powerful thighs, and his back—lean and muscled— made her pray he would turn around soon so she could catalog the rest of his killer features.

There wasn't a spare ounce of fat on him anywhere.

"Ahem." Miguel cleared his throat, winking at her as he gave his friend a head's up that she was standing here watching the Archer Show.

When he caught sight of her, he didn't bolt upright. Nope. He finished what he was doing, then gracefully unfolded himself, dropping a dozen or so snorkels and masks into the rinse tanks. The view from the front somehow managed to rival his spectacular buns.

Archer's hair stuck up, wet from his earlier plunge. In sexy disarray, it made her palms tingle with the urge to finger comb it. Then again, she might be distracted by touching the scruff of his light beard—which he definitely hadn't had the last time she'd kissed him—or following the smattering of dark fur over his chest and tight abs down to that skimpy suit hugging his hips.

Thankfully, the rinse tank kept her from eye-fucking his package.

That might have gotten embarrassing. Sunglasses to the rescue.

Especially since she was fairly sure she looked like an owl with her eyes about to pop out of her skull.

Tosin paused his class for a moment, peeking between her and Archer. Great, an audience. Just what she didn't need if things went to hell like they had the day before. She swallowed hard and mentally measured the distance between herself and the staircase. Still, she refused to run.

"Good morning," Waverly said quietly as she approached Archer.

"Morning." No *good* from him.

At least he didn't seem like he was about to explode again.

"Want some help with those?" She picked up the gallon jug of dish detergent he was about to disinfect the gear with, poured some onto one of the rags nearby, and began to scrub before he'd agreed.

"What are you doing, Waverly?" He gazed at her, pitching his voice low when he asked, clearly inquiring about a lot more than her scrub job.

She followed his lead, keeping their discussion as private as could be given the people surrounding them. "Do you think we could start over? Just pretend yesterday—hell, our whole lives before right now—never happened?"

It would simplify things, she figured.

"Can you really do that? I think it would be harder for you than for me." He scrubbed his face. "Even if you can, should you? I don't expect you to let me off easy."

She thought she'd called him on his shit pretty thoroughly yesterday. What else did he expect her to do in retaliation for losing his temper? Cane him?

An entire career spent in the midst of mostly men had conditioned her to dealing with their methods of communication or the avoidance thereof. "Um, sure. Everyone screws up. I'm not the kind of person to harp on it once amends are made."

Nor did she want to get mired down in a rehash of yesterday's bewildering argument. She didn't think she'd understand what had set him off even if he tried to explain. When she'd thought over it as she tried to fall asleep, all she could come up with for sure was that the two of them still had the capacity to affect each other deeply.

That didn't seem like a horrible thing to her.

Eventually, Archer caved. "You said *make amends*. What can I do to make it up to you?"

"Let me tag along with your snorkel group. It's been a while since I swam in tropical water like this." She'd even put on the modest one-piece suit Banks had issued as part of the uniform beneath her shorts and polo, just in case.

"Sure, I guess that's a start, though I'm certain the punishment doesn't fit the crime in this case. I thought about it a ton last night and I realized it would be even more of a dick move for me to dictate how you should feel about it." He seemed far too serious when he stared down at her. "So, I'm not joking here—whatever you want, you get."

Waverly found it odd that he kept treating her with such kid gloves. After yesterday, she didn't want to rock the boat, though. Since she wasn't pissed anymore, and he seemed to have gotten over whatever had swum up his ass, she didn't see any reason to prolong their discord.

Their arms brushed up against each other as they worked, distracting her for a moment. She stuck out her sudsy hand and said, "Truce?"

Archer swallowed hard, as if she'd given him something much more valuable than simple forgiveness. "I don't deserve that. But, yeah. Truce. Thank you."

For a while they worked together in silence, except for the squeak of their fingers on clean plastic. It wasn't awkward or strained, though. Waverly spared a few moments to take in the surroundings. They'd cruised overnight to their next destination. The beautiful beaches of Curaçao stretched out before her. Anchored a ways offshore today, they had stayed closer to prime diving locations.

Some of the guests had taken tenders to shore to explore the island. No one had plans to use the chopper. Except maybe Miguel, if he requested his ride later.

"Of all the crew, I have the fewest responsibilities." She thought about spending some quality time catching up on her reading and tanning. That would probably rock for a while, but sitting idle didn't suit her much. "I can help you out when I'm not flying. With this kind of stuff. Diving, too. Another set of eyes never hurts when you're down there."

"You're certified?"

"Want me to run down to my cabin and bring you my PADI card and logbook?" She smirked. "Of course. I traveled to a lot of excellent destinations and used leave to explore where I could. Egypt was probably my favorite. Took the Navy courses for non-diver personnel, too. Which means I'm qualified to assist dive teams or aid in search operations, though let's hope we never need one of those. Could probably blow some shit up down there in a pinch if necessary."

He blasted out a laugh. "It's so weird to me, thinking of you like that. I'll keep it in mind if we ever find ourselves in need of an explosives expert."

Waverly beamed up at him, glad that although he hadn't thought of her that way before, it didn't seem to make him like her any less. If anything, his smile and head shake led her to believe he was kind of awed. Or maybe even impressed.

By the time they'd finished the batch of gear, people had begun to wander into the staging area to prepare for their snorkel tour. Some had obviously never tried it before. So she busied herself calming those who exhibited nerves by demonstrating techniques and promising to stick close by until they got the hang of it.

Archer and Miguel were outfitting everyone with fins, masks, and snorkels, plus pool noodles or cameras or inflatable rafts, whatever they needed to feel safe and have fun. A couple of the more experienced passengers were staring longingly at the sea, getting antsy, when someone shouted, "Look, dolphins!"

Waverly rushed to the edge to ooh and ahh along with the rest of the folks gathered nearby. Sure enough, they were darting around near the ship.

"Mind if I get in? Take anyone who's ready with me before the dolphins swim off?" Waverly asked Archer, a little louder than she'd intended as excitement coursed through her.

He seemed unsure at first. "If you're comfortable…"

"I am." Would he trust her?

"Okay, go ahead. Holler if you need help."

She grinned as she stripped off her shirt and shorts then dashed over to the neat stack of equipment she'd prepared for herself. Right about then, she realized he was appraising her just like she'd done to him earlier. Hopefully he liked what he saw as much as she had.

Except when their gazes caught, he looked away, guiltily, whereas she'd only stared longer.

Then thoughts of Archer and the havoc he was wreaking on her libido vanished.

Waverly slipped on her gear and leapt into the ocean. She told the rest of the guests, "Whenever you're ready, join me."

It was a rush being in the water with animals as intelligent, agile, and predatory as dolphins. They weren't the cute cartoons most people envisioned. She was mindful of that and kept her distance, absolutely transfixed when one of the undomesticated creatures buzzed past her, whistling and clicking to its friends.

A couple of snorkelers made it in with her, chattering excitedly as they observed the pod passing by. Waverly divided her attention, making sure each of the swimmers seemed at ease with their apparatus. The salt water made it easy to stay afloat even without clutching the pool noodles some of them leaned on.

Still, sometimes it could be intimidating to jump off a perfectly good boat into endless water. She remembered the first open water swim she'd participated in on an aircraft carrier. Talk about isolation. Nothing but empty horizon in every direction she had looked.

And yet the entire ocean was their swimming pool.

Neat and terrifying at once.

Someone coughed. Waverly spun around until she identified the struggling guest. She put her face in the water and swam, cutting through the baby waves with an efficient breaststroke.

Archer must have heard the sputtering, too. Without hesitating, he executed a perfect dive off the platform and headed toward her target. The woman wasn't really in any danger. Still, instincts could sometimes trigger panic when water unexpectedly splashed you in the face or you got a swallow of it down the wrong pipe.

And *that* could kill you.

Panic, that is.

Waverly wrapped her arm around the thrashing snorkeler. "Hey. You're all right. I've got you."

She grabbed the foam pool noodle that had slipped from the woman's grasp and returned it to her. The guest clung as if it were a lifesaver.

"Tilt your face up a little, out of the chop, and take a nice deep breath," Waverly coaxed the woman.

By the time Archer emerged and shook the water from his eyes, she had the situation well under control.

He didn't try to overrule what was obviously working. Instead he floated nearby, ready to assist if needed, and let her do her job. Well, actually, he let her do *his* job. Somehow that was even more satisfying.

"I missed the dolphins." The woman sighed, then put her snorkel in her mouth, cleared it properly, and leaned forward, peeking through her mask once more.

"They may come back." Archer said, trying to cheer her up. "Besides, there are lots of other cool things to see."

He raised his hand and called the rest of their charges over to him now that the excitement was over. "We're going to split into two groups. If you just want to stick around the boat and take it easy, you'll be with Miguel. If you want to check out the reef and are up for a little swim, grab a noodle and come with me."

Waverly floundered, debating what she should do.

"Would you mind joining me?" he asked her. Then he repeated what she'd said before. "Never hurts to have another pair of eyes. Or another very capable guide."

She smiled at the compliment, then agreed.

TEN

Floating beside each other, kicking lazily, the pack of snorkelers skimmed over the reef. Archer noticed things she never would have seen from this far away, making sure to draw everyone's attention to the highlights.

Waverly couldn't wait for her next opportunity to dive. Once she'd experienced SCUBA, snorkeling didn't cut it. Not when you wanted an up-close, full-immersion experience. It was fun, just not the same.

With her eyes glued to the reef, she noticed a dark green splotch start to move in a direction contrary to the ebb and sway of the soft corals. She lifted her head high enough that she could take her snorkel out of her mouth and call, "Turtle!"

Then she held out her arm, pointing toward the creature that ascended in their general direction for a breath of air.

"Please remember not to touch it or spook it if it comes near you," Archer educated their guests. "Turtles need oxygen. We don't ever want to risk trapping it beneath the surface if it needs to breathe."

The snorkelers made room for the turtle. Their lack of threatening gestures convinced the little guy that it was okay to come closer and they all ended up scoring a better view. After their new friend had wandered off in search of his next meal, Archer steered the group back toward the *Divemaster.*

"It's funny how the turtle hardly moves its fins and yet it's still faster than me," Waverly bitched, wishing she was half as graceful in the water.

"You seem like you're doing just fine to me. Made it to that woman in a flash earlier." Warmth and pride colored his comment in return, making her stomach flutter as if she'd swallowed one of those small, schooling fish whole. "If we didn't have the group with us, I'd race you back to the boat."

"Next time." Waverly had developed her competitive side in the Navy.

When they reached the *Divemaster*, Miguel climbed aboard and began to assist people as they grew tired and exited the water. Waverly and Archer remained.

For her, she simply didn't want to leave the relaxing water any time soon.

For him, he kept an eye on every last person, making sure they got their fill of the activity safely.

Eventually, it was just the two of them, floating near the swim line that trailed behind the boat. It was ingenious. The rope had plastic bubbles spaced periodically along its length. Each end of the line was attached to one of the back corners of the boat and the slack drifted out forming a semi-circle. It acted as a corral, keeping their pool noodles, inflatable rafts, and other toys from escaping to the open ocean.

They took off their gear and piled it on the ship's platform so they could enjoy a simple swim unhindered, then collected anything else left behind by the guests as it floated within the swim line. When they were finished, he turned toward the ladder that dipped into the water off the back of the ship.

"Mind if we stay just five minutes more?" she asked him—begging, really, since swimming in the ocean alone was definitely not allowed.

"You sound like me. Nah, I could do this all day." He grinned then put his arms up on the swim line, his body rising to the surface, ankles crossed, as he stared up at the clouds overhead. Completely relaxed.

In his element.

Waverly licked her lips.

"Pretty woman. Sunshine. Ocean breeze. Have Miguel toss me a beer and I'm good for the next week or two," he elaborated.

"So, you still think I'm pretty, even though I'm not so feminine anymore?" She hated herself for asking, but the question had slipped out before she could stop it. "Can't remember the last time I wore a fancy dress or had a manicure."

He looked at her like she was crazy then. "I didn't like you for your wardrobe."

Waverly thought back on their encounters. He'd always been the aggressor. Showing her just how much he wanted her.

Now, though, he was clearly not about to budge.

Conveniently, she'd gotten a hell of a lot bolder since then.

She swam close enough that she could see the droplets sparkling like diamonds on his eyelashes.

Still, he only stared back at her. His hands never moved from that damn rope.

Why? Could it be he wasn't interested anymore?

"Would you like me if *I* kissed *you* right now?" she whispered.

"You're calling all the shots here." Archer reclined, letting the buoys do their job and keep him afloat as he lazily treaded water.

Maybe it was his thing these days to let women come to him. She had no problem with that.

"Am I?" She drifted closer still.

The wake of a passing boat finished the job, shoving her into him. Her hands landed on his bare chest. He hissed as if she'd scorched him.

Waverly peered up at him, full of mischief, and wondered if her eyes reminded him of the ocean he loved so much. He seemed like he couldn't stop looking into them. Hell, he didn't even blink. "In that case…I think I'd like to forget the past twelve years—especially yesterday—ever happened and say hello to you properly."

She wound her arms around his neck and levered against his shoulders to lift herself out of the water enough that his mouth was within reach. Gently, she pressed her lips to his and began to kiss him.

Far more patient now that he was grown, he didn't devour her in response.

Admitting that disappointed her just a little, she took it upon herself to taunt him into surrendering some of his newfound control. Waverly missed the unabashed passion he'd shared with her in those never-forgotten kisses.

She wanted this one to be every bit as memorable for them both.

When she paused, peering up to see his reaction, she didn't necessarily like what she saw. So she separated them a tiny bit.

"Isn't this weird for you?" He stared at her, worried.

"It wasn't until you asked that." She lost some of her enthusiasm. "Now it kind of is."

Still, she tried one more time to recapture their spark.

Waverly wrapped her legs around Archer's trim hips, hugging him so she didn't drown when she lost herself in the taste of salt and his mouth. His hand came up, cupping her ass to keep them steady when he returned her kiss and deepened it.

Finally!

She sucked on his tongue, teasing him into dipping inside her mouth. Hints emerged of the Archer she had known and—

Known and *wanted to fuck*, she substituted mentally.

Kiss by kiss, he grew bolder until she felt his cock start to make its presence known against the softness of her belly. There was no hiding when two thin layers of Lycra were all that separated them.

Waverly moaned—twice when he bit her bottom lip.

"You getting out, *Archie*?" Tosin called from above. When he peeked over the edge and realized why they'd suddenly gotten so quiet, he said, "Oops. Don't mind me! I didn't see anything. Much."

Backpedaling, he disappeared from view.

But the spell had been broken.

"I can't do this." Archer broke away, breathing hard.

Was it because his friend had busted them sucking face like the teenagers they'd once been?

"I'm sorry. Until we've really talked, in private, and I can apologize properly…" That again? Ugh. She'd thought they'd gotten past that, but he kept bringing it up. Killing her buzz. "Maybe not even then, Waverly. It just doesn't feel right."

Funny, it had felt perfect to her.

"Okay." She let go and swam for the ladder, hoping he hadn't glimpsed the disappointment carved on her face. The last thing she wanted was his pity.

"Wait. Don't go. Have lunch with me?" Archer asked as he climbed up behind her, probably not even taking the opportunity to check out her ass.

Silent as she swiped salt water from her legs, she debated declining. Had pretty much decided that it would be for the best if all he was going to do was knot her up inside and send her mixed signals. That would make this job hell.

"Hey," he said softly, drawing her attention back to him. "I'm sorry, okay? Just…this one time can we put it all out on the table? Then we never have to mention it again. I swear. Deal?"

Fine. "Let's get this over with."

Archer nodded. Then he used a nearby intercom to request lunch for two be served on the private sundeck off his quarters. At least they agreed about something. Interruptions would be unwelcome.

Unfortunately, she suspected they believed it for entirely different reasons.

ᕙ ELEVEN ᕚ

Waverly tried to act like it was no big deal when Archer admitted her into his personal space. Not because they were *finally* adults who could do whatever they damn well felt like. Or because they were alone in what was essentially his bedroom. But because even for former rich kids like them, this place was spec-tac-u-lar.

She twirled around in the center of the cabin, which was more like some fancy conservatory than sleeping chambers with the glass everywhere. Cover blown, probably.

He chuckled at her delight. "You haven't even seen the best part yet."

Archer waved her over to the accordion doors that essentially removed the entire wall, opening the cabin onto his own personal sundeck, complete with a double-wide lounge bed thingy, a table for two, and a jetted hot tub. She might never leave.

Wow.

"Not going to lie, it *is* pretty awesome, huh?" His smile was crooked, one corner of his lips lifting higher than the other, accenting his hawkish nose and jaw line. She thought he could pass for a slightly paler version of an Arabian prince.

"Uh huh." She nodded then sank onto one of the chairs at the table.

None too soon, either. Someone knocked.

Archer called to grant them permission to serve lunch. Maybe he was better off than that prince after all, she thought with a laugh.

"What's so funny?" he wondered aloud as their server, Maria, presented plates of cheese, meats, hardboiled eggs, and fruit. Freshly baked bread, too.

Her stomach gurgled happily at the smells wafting from the tray to her nose. She waited until they'd thanked Maria, and the woman left, before answering.

"This whole situation, really." She shrugged. "How did we go from riches to rags and back to riches? Well, I mean, not that I'm loaded, but working here is plenty good enough."

Archer sat next to her. He plucked some grapes from the assortment, popping them into his mouth. "What do you mean by that? Yeah, I walked away from my dad's fortune. But...you...how'd you end up in the military? Did your dad disapprove when you told him you wanted to join the Navy? Is that why you went rags? I have to admit, that surprised the shit out of me."

"I could tell." She remembered the utter disbelief on his face when she'd told him her name the day before. "I have no idea if my dad approves of what

I do. Or if he's proud of me. Things turned out as well as they could have, I guess. But it started out with pure desperation. I mean, in a single day my dad got locked up, my mom took the easy way out with all those pills she swallowed, and the feds seized everything we had. I'd just turned eighteen a couple of days before, so they considered me an adult. I was out on the street. On my own. I was never really close with any of the girls at school, remember? And after so many scandals, well, you know how it is. I was the drama llama. Unwelcome. Didn't have many options, to be honest."

"Time out." Archer was shaking his head. He dropped his fork and scrubbed his hands over his face. "Nothing you're saying makes sense to me. I have about twelve more questions now. Your dad did what? Your mom committed *suicide*? Jesus, Waverly! And the feds? What the fuck?"

"Oh." She tried to remember the details of the timing. With so much shit raining down on her at once, it had been kind of hard to keep up. And she hadn't even told him the worst of it yet.

That's right—he'd left soon before her life had imploded. She knew for sure because a day or two or three after someone had obviously tasted blood in the water and attacked her, knowing no one would give a fuck, she'd taken a taxi straight to Archer after being discharged, looking for help or maybe simply solace. She wasn't sure anymore.

Probably hadn't been very clear on the matter then either, given the fog that had lingered in her brain for more than a week afterward. She couldn't honestly remember much of anything. Including who had found her and taken her to the hospital in the first place. She did know it had been touch and go there for a while, so she definitely owed her life to whoever had looked out for her.

When she'd knocked on the door to the guesthouse behind Archer's father's mansion, where Archer had been staying since he'd graduated high school the year before, the door had swung open. Things were strewn about and his luggage was missing.

He'd already vanished.

That discovery had been traumatic, which was likely why she remembered the stabbing pain she'd felt then so vividly given the haziness of everything before and after it.

How she'd wished she could have gone with him wherever he'd vanished to. Hopefully somewhere a million miles away. Maybe that was what had pushed her to enlist. Or to accept the position on his ship now. It felt like coming full circle.

Archer was staring at her, waiting for her to explain.

Easy stuff first. "Turns out my dad is a sack of dog crap."

"I know the feeling," he commiserated.

"Well, mine is also a criminal. He's rotting in jail. Got busted for scamming your dad and a bunch of their friends out of millions of dollars. Everything we had became evidence in his trial and was eventually used to repay a fraction of what his victims had lost." She sighed then, finally realizing one thing that had gotten her hackles up wasn't a concern. "I guess I wondered if you freaked when you realized it was me on your team yesterday because you thought I might be untrustworthy like him."

"What?" Archer's brow scrunched. He scratched his cheek, then looked out to sea as if it was too hard to meet her stare. "No. I've only ever thought the best of you. Don't judge me by my old man. This seed fell far from that fucked-up tree. So did yours, obviously."

"I'm glad you feel that way," she admitted softly. "When I realized you had left without saying goodbye back then, I was kind of surprised myself. I thought we had something going, you know?"

"I didn't figure you'd want to see me. Or anybody, really."

Because her mother had killed herself? Or because she was mortified by her father's actions? She was growing more perplexed. He'd just admitted he hadn't known about any of that.

If he had, he would have damn well been sure she had needed a friend. Him.

That only left one other thing.

Could he know about *that*? He must. Nothing else made sense.

But how? And had her assault made him think less of her? She shoved that thought away. It had taken a long time—and a lot of counseling—to wrangle those types of insidious self-judgments and beat them into submission. She did her best. Every once in a while, her old insecurities and scars showed themselves.

She must have been quiet too long.

"I am *so* sorry, Waverly."

Oh yeah, he definitely knew. Was *that* why he'd kept his hands to himself before?

How had he found out about her attack but not her father's fuck-ups or her mother's death? Why hadn't he reached out to see if she was okay? She hadn't been. He could have made an enormous difference. Instead of allowing anger or sadness to well up, she remembered that she'd taken care of herself and put it behind her. "It was a long time ago."

"No amount of time can erase something like that."

She shrugged. "I've accepted it. Moved on as best as I can. The hardest part was not knowing—who or why, I mean. Never being able to bring my attacker to justice or simply stare him in the eye and ask how he could have been such a coward as to drug and rape a barely legal girl."

What?

Archer blinked. Suddenly it all made sense—why Waverly had come here, how she could stand to be around him.

She had no fucking clue.

Son of a bitch!

He might not have done the right thing back then, but he wasn't about to make the same mistake twice. No matter the consequences. He deserved her loathing and any other repercussions for telling the truth.

"Waverly," he croaked as bile eroded his esophagus. "I can fix that for you at least."

"What do you mean?" She tipped her head, nibbling on her lower lip.

"The man who did such a horrible thing to you...who hurt you so bad..." He drew a shaking breath, nearly crushing the tabletop in his hands, which gripped the edge as if he were clinging for dear life lest he be washed overboard in the storm brewing around them. "It was me. I'm so, *so* sorry."

Her head whipped back as if he'd sucker punched her. Then she flew from the table, knocking the chair over in her haste to escape. He wanted nothing more than to go to her, to keep her from falling as he had once in a place far, far away, but he wouldn't dare advance on her or make any moves that could be interpreted as threatening.

No wonder she'd accepted his apology so readily this morning. She hadn't even known what he'd been begging forgiveness for.

Trembling all over, pale as an albino fish's belly, she staggered away from him.

The only thing she said before she disappeared inside was, "I quit."

"I understand." Archer felt as though he'd gotten sucked into the ship's propellers where blades chopped him to bits. Nothing in him remained untouched, unscathed, or unbroken. His heart and soul were minced. Yet the only thing he cared about was Waverly.

He slapped his hand on the intercom. "Banks!"

"Archie? What's wrong?"

"It's Waverly. Find her. Help her. Whatever she needs. Tell her to take the chopper if she wants, but make damn sure she's sound to fly before you let her take off." He couldn't bear the thought of something happening to her because of him.

Again.

"Are *you* okay, Archie?"

"No." He didn't elaborate. "But Banks, anything she tells you, believe it. It's true. All of it."

He groaned as he imagined the extent of the man's shock and disappointment in him. "If you would like to go with her, I don't blame you. I'm sorry."

"Archie!"

With a vile curse, he took his hand off the intercom button. Then he locked the doors to his cabin. He wasn't fit company for anyone.

And might never be again.

A week later, Archer sat on the dive platform, dangling his legs in the ocean as he stared at the waves rolling by. He couldn't remember the last time he'd eaten, or slept, or taken a shower for that matter. Even finding the energy to dive was impossible.

He leaned forward, wondering how much farther he'd have to tilt before he slipped into the warm water and let it close over his head. It would be peaceful, he bet.

"Archie," Banks called softly.

He didn't bother to turn around or reply, annoyed that the promise of solace had been stolen from him. For now.

"We need to talk to you." Tosin this time.

"Enough is enough, man." Miguel was here, too.

Great. This was officially some sort of intervention.

He didn't bother to acknowledge them. It would never be *enough*.

They hadn't seen the devastation in Waverly's gorgeous eyes. Like the ocean on a bright day overtaken by a violent summer storm. He'd done that to her. And more.

No telling what damage he'd done by letting her kiss him. He'd been totally insane to believe she could want him after he'd abused her trust so totally.

"Tell us what happened?" Banks asked, though Archer knew it was actually a demand disguised by politeness.

He still didn't speak.

"You know, when the two of you vanished within days of each other, I actually thought she might have run off to be with you," Banks confessed. "There was something between you, wasn't there?"

"There might have been, eventually." Archer shrugged.

Shit, he hadn't meant to say that out loud.

Now that he had, though, he kept going. "I kissed her a few times. Followed her around, waiting for her to turn eighteen. Wanted to do a lot more."

Had done a whole lot more, when she'd been unable to consent.

"Ah, but you never got the chance," Banks said softly.

Archer let him think that.

"Anyway, her position here was the final one I had to fill. When her resume popped up in an online search of the top one hundred helicopter pilots in the world, I thought it was destiny. I knew she flew. I had kept tabs on her like you asked. Was aware she was making a life for herself. I just hadn't realized how good she was until I started digging in."

Archer nodded, completely unsurprised she was *that* successful at what she'd elected to do with her life. "You couldn't have known. I'm certain my father went to great lengths to keep our relationship a secret. For various reasons."

"Would you tell us more about whatever happened?" Tosin wondered as he sat next to Archer.

Miguel took the spot on his other side, then said, "We're guessing it has something to do with that crap you were spouting. About why you hated your father."

Banks sighed wearily as he sank into a deck chair. Glad he didn't have to face the man as he confessed, Archer nodded. "It does."

Maybe it would help to finally say it out loud to people who would actually listen. The one time he'd come clean, it hadn't gotten him anywhere. This would be a different kind of confession, one more about saving his soul than requesting justice be served.

No need to pretty it up.

Archer blurted out the truth: "I raped Waverly."

He dropped his face in his hands, too mortified to face his friends and the man who was more of a father to him than the one who'd knocked up his mother. If he had any tears left, he probably would have bawled. As it was, sickness gnawed at his guts.

Instead of condemning him, Banks came closer. He must have crouched behind Archer because his palm landed on Archer's back, lending him strength. "Archie, I have known you since you were three years old. There is no way you're capable of something that vile."

"Not intentionally. That doesn't mean that I didn't do it, though." He had to make them understand. "She showed up at my door one night. I knew she'd just celebrated her birthday. Hell, I'd had the date circled on my calendar for months. Was trying to decide how to approach her. She hadn't returned any of my calls or acknowledged the roses I sent her that day. So I figured she wasn't interested. I didn't know that she was occupied by her life falling apart."

"And then she came to you." Tosin smiled weakly. "I can picture her barging in with those brass balls of hers and taking what she wanted."

"Waverly wasn't really like that back then," Banks corrected him. "She was sheltered. Timid. Never encouraged by her family to explore that side of herself."

"A damn shame." Miguel cursed. "You two are starting to make me think I was better off having no parents at all than people who held me back."

He had no idea.

"Exactly, Banks." Archer turned then to meet the man's gaze briefly. "So I should have known something was up when she did exactly that."

He remembered her tearing her clothes off before she'd even made it through his foyer. Feverish and refusing to wait even until they could make it upstairs to his bedroom, she'd jumped him.

"I'm not saying this excuses my actions, but when I think back on it—as I have over and over and over—it had to have been why I didn't realize something was wrong. Remember James Trudhart?"

"Now, *that* kid was trouble," Banks muttered. "I tried to keep him away from you. He was the son your father never had, that one."

"Yeah, well, that night he'd brought over a bottle of some nasty liquor he'd stolen from his father's bar. We put away a solid amount, considering neither of us were legal yet and had never drank more than a half a glass of wine at a time during some dinner party. After he'd barfed in the flowerbeds around the pool a few times, he gave up trying to polish it off with me and staggered home. I was still pretty hammered when Waverly practically kicked my door down."

Now that he'd finally began to spill his guts, the guys let him keep going.

"Hell, I slept with her thinking she *really* was into me. That I was a sex god at nineteen, turning this virgin into the best kind of nymphomaniac. It was pretty much the highlight of my life—until way later, when I realized she hadn't just fallen into a post-sex slumber. She was unresponsive. That's when I sobered up the rest of the way. And figured out what had happened. *Who* was responsible."

"Oh God," Banks rasped. "Your father was involved, wasn't he?"

"Yep, dear old dad drugged her. Or, more likely, had someone else do it for him. He told me all about the chemical later. It was fresh on the market, the early stages of something he wanted to *invest* in. They were calling it Sex Offender. Cute, huh?" Archer held his hands up, then let them drop to his thighs.

Useless.

"Why?" Tosin, who rarely lost his temper, sounded like he might punch something.

"For years, I wasn't sure. I thought maybe he was setting me up. Getting dirt on me to keep me close and force me to do as he told. He wanted me to take over his business. I knew that wasn't the path for me. We'd fought over it. A lot."

"A *lot*," Banks confirmed.

"So after I took Waverly to the hospital and made sure she was going to pull through, I thought I'd give him the biggest fucking middle finger of all time by rejecting everything he was. His money. To me it was dirty. I didn't want any part of that. Instead, I thought I'd bring as much shame as possible to our family. I went to the police. Turned myself in." Rage filled Archer as he realized how gullible he'd been about how the world really worked.

What's right wasn't what ruled.

Greed won. Every time. Even if it was corrupt as fuck.

"Archie, no." Banks had worked for the man long enough to know where this was going.

"Yep, the officer I *confessed* to was on my dad's payroll. He didn't take a word of it onto the record and instead delivered me straight home, to my father." Here's where Archer started to get angry all over again. "And even after *all of that*, I was still stupid enough to fall for his fast-talking diversions. I was so wrapped up in what I'd done and how much I hated him that I missed the bigger picture."

"What do you mean by that?" Miguel asked for clarification.

"I thought he'd fucked me over to get me to settle down and be his bitch." He huffed, his blood pressure skyrocketing until it was a miracle he didn't keel over from a stroke right then and there. "After what Waverly told me the other day, about how her dad conned mine out of millions, I'm sure I know the truth now."

"I think you're right, son." Banks sounded as miserable as Archer felt. Even from the grave, that demon had the power to destroy things. Hurt people.

"It wasn't some kind of blackmail fodder. Or a diamond-studded leash. It was punishment." Archer groaned. "He used me to hurt Waverly. And through me, her father. An agonizing blow for any dad who actually gave a shit about his kid. Hit 'im where he's most vulnerable. How many times had he given me that bit of advice?"

"I gotta say, I was thinking you were kind of harsh with that hate business back at Windsock." Miguel spit into the sea. "Now I see you weren't ruthless enough. I hate the fuckwad, too. And everything he's done to you. This is so messed up."

"If it mattered anymore, I'd have the authorities reopen Waverly's mother's case, too. My guess is he did the same or worse to her." Banks practically vibrated with fury. "Archie, I want you to try to see this my way, okay?"

He shrugged.

"What happened was a damn tragedy. Lots of innocent people got caught in the crossfire. Yourself included."

"I'm not—"

"Be quiet until I'm finished." Banks put some steel in his tone then, making Archer, Tosin, and Miguel whip around to look at him in unison. It might have been funny if things hadn't been so damn serious. "Your father was ruthless. I admit, at first I stayed because he paid me well. Then I stayed because I loved you, and I thought I could be your advocate. In the end, I only stayed there as long as I did because I was helping the authorities build a case against him."

"You were what?" Archer almost did go overboard then. "Do you have any idea how dangerous that was?"

Banks nodded. "It was worth every risk."

"Damn, Banks. You're the man." Tosin said what Archer was thinking, and that was even before he processed the part where the guy had said he'd loved him.

Archer had to clear his throat before he could say, "Thank you."

They stared at each other for a while.

Until Miguel asked, "Why didn't the authorities crack down on Archer's dad if he was as horrible as I suspect?"

"Every time we'd get close to nailing him for some shady thing or another, he'd weasel out of it. I couldn't prove anything, but that doesn't mean I didn't know what he was up to." Banks sighed. "I would bet everything I have that he was responsible for Waverly's mother's death. And I don't doubt for a single second that his intention was not only to have Waverly's innocence stolen. How bad was she when you got to the hospital?"

"Her heart stopped three times." Archer did choke up then.

"Don't you see? You saved her life, man," Tosin grabbed him by the back of the neck and shook him as if trying to knock some sense into him.

Miguel agreed. "If it wasn't for you, she wouldn't have gone on to be a badass helicopter pilot. You gave her a second chance. A better life where she got to become the person she should have been all along. I'm not trying to say it wasn't horrible. And completely wrong. What happened to you *both*. But...you're not thinking straight about this. About her."

"You've got to go to her, Archer," Banks encouraged while Tosin and Miguel nodded. "She should hear all of this from you. Besides, she's holed up in some dump in Caracas and won't let anyone near her. She hasn't gone out for food or anything in days. I'm worried."

Shit! He couldn't let her suffer more because of him. Of course the bomb he'd dropped had shocked her, probably ripped off scabs and left her bleeding out.

Alone. In a foreign country. One that wasn't especially safe.

Considering that he'd abandoned her while wounded once, he didn't intend to fuck up like that again.

Archer climbed to his feet. "What's the fastest way to get there?"

"We had the chopper flown back onboard with a temporary replacement pilot. Give me five minutes and you can be on your way." Banks's best efforts couldn't squelch the panic bubbling up inside of Archer, now that he knew she might be in danger. "Captain Alex sent one of his officers to tail her. Not because we think she needs a babysitter or anything, but because she was upset—not thinking rationally—when she left. He can lead you to her when you get close."

"Fine. Let's go." Archer spun on his bare heel and headed for the stairs to the main deck.

"Yo, *Archie*!" Miguel called.

"Yeah?" He was tempted to spring back and hug the guys but was afraid he might lose his shit when he had something important to focus on.

"Make sure you bring our pilot back. I never did get that ride," he finished with a smirk.

"Shithead," Archer muttered, though he smiled the barest bit.

"We lurve you, too!" Tosin professed in a shout half the Caribbean had to have heard.

∾ THIRTEEN ∾

Waverly paced the dingy hotel room she'd been hiding in for a week. It wasn't a very satisfying circuit since her room was half the size of her cabin onboard the *Divemaster* and nowhere near as clean. In fact, she tried really hard not to speculate about what had caused each of the mysterious stains on the worn avocado-green rug. Her imagination was far too good for that game. Blech.

Hey, it wasn't like she had paused to consult TripAdvisor when she'd fled from Archer.

If she had been thinking rationally, things would have gone down differently. Any sort of logic had been impossible to muster in the face of the overwhelming reaction his claim had triggered. It had been emotional and primitive.

Unbearably painful.

Archer had achieved the impossible when he'd broken her heart all over again. She hadn't realized there was that much left to smash. Apparently, some kernel of her puppy love had been hiding down deep in her chest. Maybe he was right. No amount of time would heal her entirely. Especially now.

That didn't mean she planned to let this latest development shoot her down permanently.

Sure, she'd spent a solid day or two bawling her eyes out in between cursing him for making her break her no-tears edict. Then another few had been dedicated to nursing the mother of all headaches as she stared listlessly out the window at Caracas's barrios. Today, though, she'd decided enough was enough.

She had to move forward.

Get the hell out of this shithole.

If only she could decide where it was that she should go.

Waverly shushed the totally whacked part of her brain that reminded her about how the *Divemaster* wasn't so far away and that she had Banks's direct number in her phone. As betrayed as she'd felt when those unthinkable words had passed Archer's lips and blown up her world, something kept niggling her consciousness.

It could be the crazy recurring dream she'd been having. One that seemed too real to be entirely a product of her imagination. The fantasy confused her, though, because it didn't mesh with what she now knew had happened. In the vision, she and Archer were young again and making love. Frantic, reckless sex. But definitely something mutually enjoyable. *Very* enjoyable.

How could her mind romanticize her own attacker?

Maybe she knew where to go after all, straight to her therapist's waiting room.

Because trying to puzzle out how her subconscious could still so desperately want Archer that it manufactured pleasurable memories to cover up the awful ones...it made her feel like her own mind was violating her.

Or was it?

What if her dreams were actually rooted in memories she hadn't been able to recall?

What if Archer had misrepresented what had happened?

Had she really understood what he'd said to her or why he would have bothered to rape her when she would have gladly slept with him of her own volition?

No.

Something wasn't making sense, but she couldn't work it out on her own.

As it had since the sun rose through her dirty window this morning, her brain attempted to reengage. She couldn't quite force her thoughts to coalesce into whatever epiphany she felt brewing, but maybe that was because she hadn't had a decent meal in a while.

Or even a cup of tea to jumpstart herself.

Mmm, tea.

Promising her rumbling stomach she would do a better job of taking care of it today, she hoisted her suitcase onto the bed and began to gather her belongings.

She'd gotten about halfway there—she didn't have much—when someone pounded on the door. *"Privacidad, por favor."* She requested to be left alone, as she had every other time the maid came by to do what she could with the place.

"I have no idea what you just said. Open the door, would you?"

Archer! What the fuck was he doing here?

She stood staring incredulously at the entrance to the room when he started banging again. "Come on, Waverly. Please. I need to talk to you."

Should she? Shouldn't she?

While she debated, he thumped his fist on the flimsy barrier one time too many. The door ripped off one of its hinges and hung so she could see him through a wedge-shaped gap. His hand hovered in the air, mid-knock.

The shock on his face and the utter absurdity of the situation pushed her over the edge. She couldn't take her eyes off his horrified expression while he glanced repeatedly between her and the busted door.

Then, together, they burst out laughing.

"Going somewhere?" he asked, eyeing her open suitcase and the fistful of dirty laundry she'd been about to stuff into the front pocket to segregate it from the few remaining clean items she had left.

Just like that, her amusement evaporated. "Not your business."

"I feel like an idiot out here." He tried to pry the door open from the outside. It only cracked more. "Would you please let me in? If you don't feel safe alone with me, then maybe could I have a few minutes of your time somewhere public? It's just that...I think you'd rather not have anyone overhear what I'd like to tell you."

Waverly dropped her clothes and picked up one of the other items inside her suitcase instead. Without warning or hesitation, she spread her legs, raised her arms, and aimed her pistol slightly off from his face. Enough to scare him, but not actually on target. Besides, he didn't have to know it was unloaded at the moment. "I can take care of myself these days. Why don't you start talking?"

"Jesus Christ!" He ducked behind the ruined door, as if that would stop a bullet when it hadn't been able to handle the impact of his fist. "Waverly, chill out. I'll stay in the hall. I just thought you deserved to know what happened that night, okay?"

That made her pause.

It had eaten at her, not knowing all those years.

And he didn't *have* to enlighten her. Hell, he hadn't had to confess to being her attacker either.

There it was. The thing that had been bugging her all morning.

Why *had* he done that?

Guilty conscience? Maybe, but if so, spilling his guts obviously hadn't worked because here he was, looking as distraught as he had when he'd confessed to her.

"Waverly?" he asked again, probably expecting her to turn him into Swiss cheese any second.

Instead, she crossed the room, straightened the door as best she could, then yanked the handle.

It was a teensy bit fun to see him jerk in surprise. Evil, yet satisfying.

"You're responsible for getting this fixed. It's not going on my bill." She shook her head at him as she wandered back to the rumpled bed and plopped down, placing the gun within easy reach on the nightstand. It might not have any ammo in it, but she could always hit him with it, if it came to that.

"I'm good for it." He shrugged. "I told Banks to give my money to charities, but he keeps finding ways to squirrel away emergency funds here or there for me and forgetting to mention it until later."

"He's a good man."

"The best." He nodded.

Since you've officially lost the crown, she added mentally.

"So…you want to kick me out of a chopper at five thousand feet above shark-infested waters or something?" He cursed then. "I don't blame you, honestly. But you should know that I hate myself enough for both of us because of what I did to you."

"Nah. The US military doesn't condone torture, Archer. I'd take you out quickly."

"Are you actually cracking a joke right now?" He groaned, "Waverly—"

"Stop. Get to what you came here to say. I don't have a lot of patience left." She rubbed her shirt between her fingers, nervous as fuck that he might be about to impart knowledge more deadly than her pistol.

He closed his eyes for a couple of seconds. When he opened them again, he went straight to the point. "My father drugged you with some designer libido-enhancing substance. I didn't know. You showed up at my door and morphed into a fantasy come to life. Telling me you wanted to get with me, and that you were legal now. All I could think was how beautiful you were, how untamed under all your shyness. I was kind of drunk, though I'm not saying I shouldn't have realized something was off. I—"

He swallowed hard, his eyes turning glassy.

A flash of memory blazed to the front of her mind. She grabbed her skull and folded in half, putting her head between her knees. Her dreams. They weren't dreams at all.

It *had* happened like that.

"Waverly!" he shouted then ran to her, dropping to his knees at her feet. His hands reached for her, but he stopped before making contact.

Would he be so considerate of her boundaries if he was some kind of sexual predator?

She might have wondered more about that if his explanation hadn't unlocked something subliminal. It was like trying to watch TV when the signal was nearly non-existent. All she could make out was the faintest of images through the static. "We fucked on your entryway floor."

"Yeah. Then the stairs. And a few other places as I tried to get us to my bedroom." He rested his forehead on her knee then.

Automatically, her fingers sank into his hair, soothing him, though the gesture also brought her comfort.

He kept going, describing the whole night, in detail, painting a picture of everything she'd missed that matched the glimpses she'd gotten while sleeping. She hadn't said a peep about them, so there was no way he could have lied and yet described everything she had recalled—not knowing that's what she'd done.

Things were finally beginning to make sense.

When he got to the end of his story, he cringed. "I didn't know what I was doing to you, that you weren't yourself. Until you slipped into unconsciousness."

"*You* took me to the hospital."

"Of course! You almost died in my arms!" He lifted his face toward hers then, his eyes bloodshot.

This time her heart found an entirely new way to break.

For them both.

Because it was painfully obvious what had happened. Like a lightning strike, the pieces of the puzzle he'd given her aligned, lighting up her world in an instant. "Archer, your father used you. To hurt my father. It was ruthless revenge. You and I, we were both pawns. Well, maybe *weapons* is a better way to put it."

"I know. I realized that after you told me about what had happened between them." He groaned. "All that time, I had no clue."

"That means, Archer, that you were violated as surely as I was."

He froze. "Huh?"

"They made you do something against your will. Worse, something that violated the core of who you are. I've had years of counseling to help me cope with what happened. You haven't been able to come to terms with it at all, have you?" When he didn't respond, she reached out and cupped his cheek, brushing away the single drop of moisture trailing down the strong bones. "I can't imagine what that's done to you. Or how you've survived."

"You...you don't hate me?"

"I hate your father. And mine."

"That makes two of us," he snarled.

"It's going to take me a while to think all of this through. Rewrite history again in my mind. But how could I blame you, Archer? I can't. Not after what you've shared, the tiny bits I can remember, and what my gut is telling me. You know what's pissing me off more than anything right now?"

"Hopefully, not me for once." He smiled faintly at her.

"No. Well, not really." She shook her head and he frowned. "I mean, it's that not only did they use us, but they also stole my memories of my first time. Something I'd looked forward to sharing with you for a really long time. Was it awesome?"

"Right up until I realized you were in some kind of coma, barely breathing." He looked like he might break more shit then.

"But before that…"

"It was incredible. *You* were incredible." Archer brushed his thumb over her lower lip and she couldn't help but suck it into her mouth and nip the pad before he withdrew.

"That fucker made me believe some fiend took my virginity, when I'd hoped to give it to you all along. They erased the knowledge that it was you I shared that night with and replaced it with horror. Bone-deep terror. That I might have been exposed to diseases. Violated by someone I'd never consent to a relationship with. They spoiled my joy and made me afraid of something that probably was magnificent. *That's* what's making me furious." Waverly's hands shook and she got more fired up by the second. "I hate what they did to you. And that they ruined any chance the two of us had of getting together."

Archer changed before her eyes. His grief took on a bitter edge. Then pure fury hardened his features. "You're right. They robbed us of that, too. All these years we spent apart, it hasn't changed the chemistry between us. We might have been happy together. Had a family. Made a life. And now we'll never know if we could have."

Another thing she would mourn forever.

Waverly put her hands on his shoulders, then skimmed down his arms until she clasped his hands in hers. He squeezed in return, giving her the courage to say, "We can't go back. But maybe sometime you'll give me an instant replay of what I missed?"

"You'd want that?" Undiluted sexiness. That's the only way she could think of to describe the look he shot her then. His eyes blazed and his lips parted. His pupils dilated as he leaned closer.

"Uh huh." She nodded.

"I need to hear you say it. Clearly, Waverly. No mix-ups this time."

"I would love to finally know what it feels like to have you inside me, Archer. Where you've always belonged." Well, there was no going back from a statement like that.

Except he didn't say anything. Didn't even seem to breathe.

The stress of the week hit her then, sapping the last of her strength and energy. She thought longingly of the *Divemaster* and his circular bed, surrounded by all those windows. A place of light, and beauty, and safety.

And food.

Courses and courses of gourmet chow.

She cleared her throat, but he was still staring at her with that powerful gaze, processing her statement.

"Can we go now?" The sooner they left here, the sooner they'd be back there.

They could stay locked up there for the next week, fooling around, sleeping, making up for lost time, and gorging on desserts prepared by the pastry chef she'd been standing next to at their staff meeting, which seemed like a lifetime ago.

It sounded like heaven to her right then.

"Nope. We're staying a little while longer." He launched to his feet, then crossed to the door in two long strides. Without straining, he grabbed the dresser next to the entrance and heaved it in front of the broken wood, propping it into place while barricading them inside.

Then he strode back toward her, whipping his T-shirt over his head as he did.

Waverly's heart somersaulted in her chest. "Does that mean you'll show me what I missed? Give me that, at least."

"Hmm..." He wiggled his brows. "Yes. I think I will. *If* you'll agree to come back to your job as soon as we're finished with this demonstration."

"Done." She shoved out her hand.

He shook it, but didn't let go.

The warmth of his palm on hers had her melting already.

Archer used their connection to tug her up and into his arms, nuzzling the side of her face as he whispered, "I hope you know I'm only teasing if you decide you don't want the position anymore. I'd do anything to make this up to you. To set it right, as best I can. Making love to you would be an honor. One I don't deserve. Except I'm not a good enough man to turn you down."

"Then let's do this."

Waverly wasn't about to wait for Archer to change his mind.

Or for her to lose her nerve.

She wrapped her arms around him, stroking the exposed skin of his back as if she were petting some powerful animal. It probably would bum him out if she admitted she was imagining something along the lines of the jaguars prowling through the jungles surrounding them rather than one of his beloved sea creatures.

Although he did seem to have something in common with a swordfish at the moment. Maybe she'd share her nickname with him some other time. One not so incredibly crucial for them both. Laughing now would probably bruise his ego. The fact that she could even loosen up enough to have thoughts like those amazed her.

And reinforced her belief that this was absolutely the right thing to do.

The two of them had always meshed. Had fun together. Been attracted to each other from the first moment she'd been capable of experiencing those feelings for another human being. It had been him she measured other men against. And they'd always disappointed. Not their fault. He was just…special.

Archer surprised her, seeming to be caught in the same current she was. Instead of ridding her of her clothes immediately, he cradled her against his chest for a minute, swaying in time to some slow music only he could hear while he stroked her hair, and then kissed the top of her head. She felt cherished and protected.

Two things that only turned her on more.

"Kiss me," she murmured against his collarbone. "Like you used to."

"How about if I do it better than back then?"

"I'd like to see you try." She grinned, or would have if he hadn't curled an index finger below her chin, tipped her face toward his, then descended, fusing his mouth to hers.

Softly at first, with tiny sips that left her room to suck in breath between them. Quickly, though, their tenderness morphed into something more urgent. He cupped the back of her neck and held her in place so that he could situate his mouth to allow it to fit tighter to hers. His tongue fluttered over the seam of her lips and she opened to him.

One of his hands dropped to her ass, pulling her flat against his body so she couldn't ignore how turned on he truly was. His cock impressed her—thick and long between them.

"Is that okay?" he paused to ask.

"No," she gasped.

He froze.

"More," she demanded, tired of waiting for the real thing. "Take your time later. Right now I want it like you said it was. Wild. Frantic. Desperate."

Because that's how she felt knowing she was about to have something she'd dreamed of for as long as she could remember.

"I'm not normally a slow-and-steady-missionary kind of lover. Though sweet sex doesn't sound half bad when I'm thinking of doing it with you." He balked. "Are you sure it's a good idea for all of me to come out and play right now?"

"Absolutely." She smiled then went onto her tiptoes for one final sweet taste of him. "I want you for who you are, Archer. Not for who you think I need you to be."

He nodded at her as he evaluated her sincerity close up.

Then he walked until the backs of her knees hit the bed. He kept advancing, pressing her backward until she bounced onto the mattress and he followed her down.

That's when clothes started flying—his shorts, her shirt. Archer toed off his sneakers, letting them drop to the floor, followed by his socks. Finally, she wormed out of her pajama pants.

Good thing she hadn't bothered to put on a bra or panties yet today.

Saved time.

"You're even more beautiful now," he rasped before he sampled her exposed body. First a lick on her collarbone, then a suck on one breast, followed by a pet between her legs. It was as if he didn't know where to start first.

She could understand. Because while he lit up nerve endings all over her body with his random introductory touches, she was studying his body.

Yes, she'd seen nearly all of it the other day.

But it was different to observe him in motion, hovering over her, about to devour her.

Of all the things it made her feel to watch his power, grace, and strength, *frightened* was not one of them. Not even close.

Waverly returned the favor, groping every inch of him she could reach, wanting to catalog it in case she never got this lucky again. It was frenetic. Fevered. And honest.

When Archer rose, she took the opportunity to surge forward and crash their mouths together for another round of making out. This was no clandestine peck, though. Nothing like the innocent kisses they'd shared as teenagers.

It seared her from the inside out.

He groaned into her mouth and dropped lower, squashing her in the best of ways. She spread her thighs so his hips could rest between them. The rest was magic.

His erection aligned with her center.

A swing of his hips had the tip of his cock prodding her entrance. It was as if he was knocking so she would admit him.

"Son of a bitch!" he shouted, his head tipping back to expose the tendons in his neck. She couldn't resist taking a love bite out of one. Until she registered his regret and the slight shift of his lower body.

Away from hers.

Fuck that.

She arched up to maintain contact, though it wasn't as steady a pressure as she needed.

"Waverly. Wait," he commanded between gritted teeth. "I don't have protection. Definitely didn't expect our conversation to go like *this*."

Oh. Well, at least he'd thought of it. All her common sense had flown out the window around the time he took his shirt off. There was no way she was stopping short of the goal here. "Banks made each of the crew members get a full physical workup. I'm clean. And on birth control."

"I'm clean, too."

She nodded. "Then why are we wasting time talking?"

"Seriously, you trust me?"

"Would I be letting you fuck me in the first place if I didn't?" She gave him a pass since there was some serious diversion of blood flow from his brain to his cock at the moment.

He gave her a curt nod. "Right."

Then he didn't waste another moment. He took his erection in hand and rubbed it over her mound, making her moan and writhe. Especially when he used the fat head to separate her pussy lips and rode the furrow up until he prodded her clit a few times for good measure.

He went one step beyond when he grasped his shaft then slapped his dick on her pussy, the vibrations making her mewl and forget about attempting to say anything coherent. Even more thrilling was the way it made her feel...owned.

"Inside. Now." She planted her hands on his hips, loving the flex of his ass beneath her fingers, which rested on the upper swells of his tight muscles. Using her grip on his slim waist, she drew him closer, taking initiative in driving his cock within her the barest bit.

It had been a while since she'd indulged in sex with a real live partner. He had her vibrator beat both in length and girth. So when he wedged inside her, it took some adjusting to make him fit.

"Shh." He held her still as he worked into her pussy bit by bit. "I'm gonna give you all of me, don't you worry about that. Just let me take care of you. My way."

When she relaxed, he slipped another few inches deeper within her.

They both groaned.

"That's right. Take me."

She did.

So he kept giving.

Each time she thought they couldn't possibly be connected any tighter, he showed her that they could. With every push and retreat, he simultaneously stoked her lust and delivered additional pleasure.

And that was before he even really began to thrust.

Archer smothered her with kisses. He supported himself on his forearms, which were braced somewhere near her shoulders. His fingertips caressed her cheeks while he rippled his body above her, making contact with her breasts, belly, and pelvis.

Then he did it faster.

Harder.

With a wicked twist that pressed his abdomen against her clit in the most delicious way possible. It was at that precise moment that Waverly realized exactly how badly she'd underestimated him and his abilities as a lover.

"How the hell can I not remember this?" She moaned and hugged him tighter, probably scratching the shit out of his back in the process. He didn't seem to mind.

"While *you* blew my mind, I probably wasn't this great in bed back then. I've learned a few tricks in the past decade." Unapologetically sexy, he demonstrated one or two then, sucking on her neck somewhere below her ear as he ground his pelvis against *exactly* the right place to make her spasm around him.

"Not sure I caught that one. Better show me again," she panted.

He did.

Repeatedly.

"Oh, fuck!" she screamed. "Archer!"

"Am I hurting you?" His stride hitched then, making his cock slip from her pussy. "*Scaring* you?"

"Only because you stopped. Now I'm afraid you might leave me hanging. Get back in there and finish the job."

"I'm not used to taking orders when I'm fucking, Waverly." Something in his stare made her shivery at the revelation.

It wasn't threatening when he admitted it. It was exhilarating.

"Then I guess you'd better do something to shut me up. You know, like fuck me some more. Harder." She didn't know where these suggestions were coming from. They weren't like her either.

Though he plunged back inside her body and rode her furiously, her plan backfired.

Instead of keeping her quiet, his jackhammering hips only made her more vocal.

Waverly put one arm over her head, palming the headboard to keep him from shoving her into the wall with his frenzied fucking. She cried his name over and over.

Pleaded for him to get her off.

For all she knew, she might have begged him to marry her if it meant he'd do this with her every day of their lives. There was no telling what he drew out of her during those impossibly long minutes. One thing was certain, though—it was something that no one else had ever evoked.

The next time he kissed her, she knew she was going to shatter.

She tightened around his stroking shaft, trying to keep him as deep within her as possible. Sweat slicked his chest, making him glide over her.

And when she felt the first flutters of orgasm, she called to him.

"Yes, that's it. Come for me, Waverly," he grunted. "I'm right there with you. Going to fill you so full. Fuck."

Who knew dirty talk did it for her?

Archer did, now.

She drummed her heels on the bed as she flew apart, afraid that she might never recover from bliss this complete. Her heart nearly exploded in her chest when he began to shoot deep in her pussy, branding her with the rush of his come.

Feeling him share this ecstasy with her set her off again. She wrung him dry.

Archer collapsed onto his back, making the entire bed shake as if there had been an earthquake. Then he patted his heaving chest, calling her to him. She gladly went, cuddling into the crook of his arm. Her head rested perfectly on his shoulder and she slung a thigh over his. He kissed her forehead then lay still, recovering.

It took a few minutes before she could even think straight again. What they'd shared hadn't been perfect, or careful, or planned. It had been authentic. An outpouring of relief and passion that had been stored up for years.

Of course, it was also exhausting.

When she became aware of their surroundings, she wanted nothing more than to pack up and leave so they could do this all over again. Somewhere not so creepy.

"I have to admit. I never pictured my first time—actually, second, I guess—with you going down in a place like this." Waverly chuckled as she glanced around at the yellowed wallpaper, which peeled up at the corners.

"Try not to look. Next time we do it in a hotel, I'll make the reservations." He put his hand over her eyes and drew her closer still.

"Yeah, right. You'll ask Banks for help."

"Even better idea."

Waverly snuggled against him, sighing in bone-deep contentment.

She stayed there, utterly relaxed, until her body refused to listen to her brain's demands any longer.

"Archer?" she mumbled on a groan, hating to ruin the moment.

"Hmm?" He sounded half-asleep. Content and relaxed in a way she never remembered seeing him before, unless it had been for a split second when he reclined on the swim line after their snorkel last week.

Her stomach protested. Loudly. "I'm *starving*."

"I don't suppose this place has edible room service?" he sighed.

"Negative." She shook her head, sending her hair flying.

He ran his fingers through the messy waves and smiled softly at her. "You're so fine. Leave your hair down from now on. Loose, like this. It suits you."

"Thanks." She shoved him off the edge of the bed. "Now get up. Before you give me any ideas. Because I'm seriously going to pass out if you don't feed me soon."

Archer growled. "Oh, I'll feed you all right. Once we're back on the ship."

Though she realized he wasn't talking about lunch, she couldn't help but ask, "How long is that going to take? Can I swing by McDonald's or whatever the equivalent is here on our way to the airport?" Honestly, she didn't recall from her harried trip here. Her mind had blanked.

"I'll buy you a whole damn restaurant chain of your own if you get it to go." He eyed her with an entirely different sort of hunger. "I'm going to be hard again before we even make it there. I don't suppose road head is an option when you're the pilot, huh?"

"Sky head," she corrected as they yanked their clothes on nearly as fast as they'd shed them. "And sorry, no."

"That's all right. I'll entertain myself by watching you handle the stick and being jealous." He grinned.

Just then, Waverly heard voices outside the broken door. Maybe someone on staff had noticed the damage. Oops.

Except they weren't speaking Spanish.

Archer noticed that, too. He put his finger over his lips and stepped between her and the door.

Without wasting a second, Waverly grabbed the gun off the nightstand and unpacked her bullets. She had not found Archer again, and begun to make things right, just to get jumped by some street thugs who might do more than steal their wallets.

Archer was wealthy. That made him a target wherever he went.

Confirming her suspicions, the dresser rocked. They were trying to get in.

∽ FIFTEEN ∽

"**Y**ou need anything else out of there?" Archer pointed to her suitcase.

"No."

"Then I think we're going to have to go out the back way." He lifted his chin toward the rickety fire escape outside the window. At least it had that.

She nodded.

They hadn't made it there before the door splintered and two guys toppled in over the tipped furniture.

"Get the window open!" he shouted. No use for subtlety now. "I'll take care of them."

She thought that was an odd call given that she was holding a gun, but there wasn't any time to sit there and bicker. So she yanked on the window.

Painted shut, of course.

Waverly wrapped one of her discarded shirts around her fist and the pistol, then smashed the window as she'd been taught. She knocked out the remaining glass as best she could, then turned back to Archer. He had a mean right hook, she noted, as if this were just another training maneuver.

Shaking off shards of glass and the shirt covering her weapon, she leveled it at the intruders.

"Stop!" she shouted. "Or I *will* shoot."

They hesitated long enough for Archer to sprint to the window and dive out, testing the rusty fire escape. Fortunately, it held. He stuck his hand through the opening a moment later and helped her climb through with only minor scratches.

When they hit the street level, they ran around to the front of the hotel, screaming for Captain Alex's officer to get his ass in gear. To his credit, he didn't ask questions, simply kept up as they made their way to the rental car Archer had left in the lot across the street.

He drove. She sat shotgun, her pistol ready yet held out of sight as they tore down the street toward the airport.

"Guys?" The officer tried a few times to buckle his seatbelt then gave up as Archer flew around corners like he was driving that Lamborghini Banks had promised him.

"Did you see two men come inside just now? One about my height, the other six inches shorter? Both on the bruiser side of the spectrum?"

"Uh...maybe?" the officer, Ted, stammered.

What was up with that?

Was he in on whatever had almost happened? Or had he been sleeping on the job?

Archer looked at her, shooting her a look that clearly said *stay alert*.

Yep. No problem there.

She probably had enough adrenaline in her system between the orgasms he'd given her and the scare the bad guys had given her to keep her awake for a week. Her fingers drummed on her knee.

After ten miles, winding through dense city streets, Archer slowed. There hadn't been a single sign of the guys from the hotel or any other pursuit, so they started to relax. At least she calmed down from, say, a nine-point-five on the Oh Shit scale to a solid seven.

Bad luck? Could be. Nothing to completely freak out about. Right?

Waverly laughed internally at that. How fucked up did your life have to be that after having your afterglow snuffed out by muggers you thought hey, that wasn't so awful?

"What's funny about this?" Archer threw up one hand while the other guided the car proficiently through traffic. He was a great driver.

That had her squirming in her seat.

He peered at her weapon, shaking his head.

"Are you intimated by the size of my gun, Archer?" She spared a glance at him, lifting one brow dramatically.

"Only when you aim it at me." Now he was laughing, too. "You know this is not normal right? You're not supposed to enjoy yourself when you're being chased by thugs."

"Eh. I've lived through worse."

He slid his free hand to her and squeezed her thigh before returning it to the wheel. Then he addressed the bewildered and slightly green officer in the backseat. "Hey, Ted. Get Banks on the phone. Tell him you're going to need a ride home in a second chopper since ours is a two-seater. You'll have to take it to Aruba, and we'll send a tender in for you, since Waverly will be on our pad. Make sure he has something ready for her to eat as soon as we land. Also, I need him to settle up Waverly's hotel bill and pay for some damage."

The guy nodded and took care of the details.

Waverly almost mentioned that she could make two trips to transport Archer and then Ted, but she figured it was for the best if she didn't. Obviously that was where Archer was going with this, too.

But was he concerned for her or did he want her to himself when they got back?

She figured she knew the answer to that when he only stopped long enough to clean out the mini bags of peanuts from a vending machine in the crew lounge at the private airport before hustling her out onto the launch pad. "Let's get you the hell away from here."

When they were safely tucked into his helicopter, she paused to toss back a few handfuls of the snack he'd given her. With her mouth full of nuts, she said, "Mmm, salty. Probably not the kind you imagined me eating when you asked about sky head, huh?"

Though he laughed, he was still tense, so she tried again.

"Feel free to show me how you handle your stick while I play with this one." She winked at him as she fired up the engines.

It might have sounded flippant, but if she didn't joke, she might freak out. What the hell was happening? Who would have thought active duty would have been less dramatic than retirement?

"Definitely no distractions today. Take us home, please, Waverly."

Once they were airborne, she took a moment to appreciate the view. It never failed to amaze her.

Archer had the sea. *This* was her world, and she loved it every bit as much.

"How mad is Miguel going to be that you got to fly with me before he did?" she asked over the headset as they picked up speed, flying directly toward the ever-changing coordinates sent to her by the *Divemaster's* systems.

Landing on a moving target was always an exciting challenge. One she was more than capable of executing even in her current condition.

"He'll probably get over it by the time we turn fifty." Archer didn't seem too disturbed.

Miles of gorgeous blue water streaked beneath them as they raced back to the *Divemaster.* Lost in the familiar rhythm of flying and the gorgeous landscape they zipped through, Waverly felt like their trip had just begun when her instruments told her the *Divemaster* would be in sight any moment.

Archer finally broke the silence. "I've never seen something up top come close to being as beautiful as what I see underwater." When she glanced over, he wasn't looking at the spectacular scenery or the megayacht where he did good while having fun.

He was staring at her.

～ SIXTEEN ～

"**D**o you still need me to fly you somewhere this afternoon?" Waverly asked the next day as she emerged from their over-the-top bathroom, which could easily have passed for a high-end spa. Funny, he didn't think of it as his quarters anymore. Overnight, she'd changed his perspective on everything.

It felt right when she shared his space. Less lonesome and wasteful.

For the first time, he found himself actually enjoying the deluxe appointments, proud he could ensure her comfort and pamper her as she deserved.

Naked, she tipped her upper body to one side so to blot water from the long length of her hair with a thick towel. The motion put her perfect-handful breasts and the soft dip of her waist on display. She didn't resemble models he'd seen in either fashion or jack-off mags. Not overly voluptuous or stick-thin, either.

That didn't matter. To him, she was the ideal woman. Her fit and healthy proportions had him regretting his decision not to shower with her. Except he'd had to finish arranging some final details before they left.

"Yeah, if you don't mind." He made sure she couldn't see his face when he replied. Didn't want to give any of his plans away. Unlike most people, she knew him well enough to recognize when he wasn't being entirely upfront.

She laughed. "You're the boss, Archer. Literally."

"Should I fire you?" he asked, in all seriousness. It had been weighing on his mind as the connection between them strengthened, turning into something precious that he was afraid to sever with bullshit like this. "I mean, I don't want you to think of me as your employer. We're equals, Waverly. In our relationship, and in what we do here on the *Divemaster*."

"It's up to you." She strolled over to him then, probably intending to use her nudity to her advantage, though he didn't mind. It was a highly effective strategy. After placing a quick kiss on his cheek, she said. "Let me put it this way...you know how even if you never got paid for it, you'd keep diving?"

He nodded, reaching for her hip.

She slapped his fingers away then abandoned him in favor of rummaging through the dresser, which also meant her ass was on display for him to ogle. Banks had waved his fairy godfather wand or something, sending one of the housekeeping staff on a shopping spree at his request. They'd stocked her wardrobe with sundresses, bikinis, and killer underwear so she had selections beyond her Banks Foundation uniform.

"Archer?"

He had to think back for a moment as he watched her shimmy into a skimpy pair of panties. He was going to order Banks to give himself a giant Christmas bonus this year. "Yes? Of course, I love diving. Doing it for a living was really just a way to survive while I did what I wanted anyway."

"Flying is the same for me. Except I need an aircraft to pilot. So as long as you supply that, I'll gladly schlep you anywhere you want to go. Because it means I get to do what I love most." She smiled slowly at him then as she finished clasping the bra he already couldn't wait to peel off her later. "Make that *second* most."

It was going to be harder than he had thought to keep his hands to himself until they arrived at their destination.

"Okay. If you're going to do the work regardless, you deserve to be paid for it. But I need you to understand that I don't see you as hired help. In fact…" An idea came to him then.

"Yes?"

"How about you ditch that uniform? I feel kind of sleazy lusting after you when you're wearing it." He wouldn't tell her about his true stroke of genius until he'd already made it official. That way, she couldn't argue. Or refuse.

"I bet you wouldn't complain if I found a French maid outfit in here, though."

Archer thought of her in seamed stockings. He'd bend her over, flip up her skirt, and… "Banks didn't really put one in there, did he?"

"No!" She slapped her hand over her mouth. "But I bet one of the housekeeping staff has a feather duster I could borrow when we get back."

If they had enough energy for roleplaying tonight, it would probably mean his plan had been an epic failure. "We'll see."

"Where's your sense of adventure?" she asked him as she ducked into a short, silky dress that looked like an oversized handkerchief. It left her sexy legs—and a good amount of her cleavage—exposed. Fine by him.

Hell, he'd have no problem with her walking around naked all the time.

Maybe he'd have to talk to Banks about filling one of their tours with nudists.

"Ready?" he asked, eager to be on their way.

She plucked her sunglasses and a big floppy hat from a table near the door, then said, "Yep. Where am I taking you anyway?"

"There's a small group of people subsistence living not too far from here. One of the other arms of the Banks Foundation will be supporting indigenous people who would rather continue their traditions than modernize. Since we're in the area anyway, we're going to take some supplies and medical aid over to them."

"Sounds good to me. Not that different than what I used to do in the Navy sometimes." Waverly shot him a stare so full of warmth he felt it heat his entire body. This time it wasn't the lusty sort either. Or not only that. It was something more profound.

"What?" he asked as he opened the door and ushered her out.

"Think of how many people in the world are going to be impacted positively because of you." She linked her arm with his as they wound their way through the yacht on their path to the helipad.

He shrugged, kind of uncomfortable with that assessment. "It's not because of *me*. It's because of my father's money. Considering how many people probably suffered or were fucked over so he could amass that pile of cash, it seems only right."

"Even so, we both know that just because something *should* happen doesn't mean it *will* happen." She turned him toward her, then pulled him down for a long, lingering kiss. "You're really doing it, Archer. Making this happen."

"All I did was sign a bunch of papers. Banks is the hero, not me."

She whispered up at him then, thinking about how he'd saved her more than a decade ago even if she hadn't known it then. "You'll always be my hero."

"I'll do my best for you, Waverly."

With a pat on his cheek, she turned and they continued walking in no hurry, pausing in several of the common areas to talk to passengers who'd gone diving with him over the past few weeks and waved hello to others they were also coming to know from shared meals or simply living on the *Divemaster* together for a while.

As a freelance divemaster, Archer's clients usually hadn't stuck around more than a week or two at most. Though some came back year after year to the same resorts, he, Tosin, and Miguel hadn't been there the next time they returned.

This was different. He was learning about each of the people temporarily living onboard and coming to care, especially when they shared some of the heartbreaking details of their loved ones' health crises.

It made them more real to him. More than tourists passing through.

He was starting to feel like his nomad days were over. Sure, the *Divemaster* moved for him. But he could no longer imagine himself leaving her behind for another place he couldn't grow some roots.

It would be kind of sad when the passengers who'd taken this maiden voyage with them switched out with the next group of guests. Then again, it was wonderful to see how much they'd relaxed in the time they'd been onboard. How many more smiles were exchanged than when they'd first arrived.

Some of the passengers had taken it upon themselves, with help from Banks, to organize their own support group meetings in the evenings and had plans to start up a virtual edition on social media so they could keep in touch after they went home. One good deed expanded and grew, picking up momentum as it went.

Archer thought they might actually be making a difference, however small, in these people's lives, and he couldn't wait to see who Banks would bring in next and what they could do to help them.

Caught in an introspective mood, he soon found himself relaxing in the passenger seat of the helicopter as Waverly did her thing. He didn't feel the need to scrutinize her or ask if she felt everything was okay. He was like the blissfully ignorant subset of clients who'd relied on him to lead their dives.

He trusted her, absolutely, with his life.

So he didn't bug her before or during takeoff, limiting his glances in her direction to the ones he needed to keep his stiffening dick happy.

"I wonder if I'm going to have a hard-on every time I fly with you. So far we're two for two." He might have caught her off guard with that statement, but though she risked a glimpse at the tent in his shorts, she didn't so much as bobble the stick. "It's sexy, watching you like this. Confident, competent, totally badass. Miguel was right about that."

"Thanks, Archer." She flashed him one of her dazzling smiles as they began to accelerate toward their target. "That might be the sweetest thing anyone's ever said to me."

He was saved from responding when a charcoal wedge appeared on the horizon. It grew bigger as they flew in that direction.

"Is that someone from the *Divemaster*?" She pointed at what turned out to be a Zodiac—an inflatable motorboat—which bounced along the waves, hauling ass in the opposite direction from where they were headed.

Considering they were out in the middle of nowhere, relatively, he figured it wouldn't make any sense to deny it. He grunted, thinking they'd cut things close. "Yeah. I think it's Tosin and Miguel. They said something about going fishing earlier."

"I wonder why they didn't cast off the yacht." She shrugged.

Because they hadn't really been fishing. Archer crossed his fingers and hoped she wouldn't be pissed at him when she realized that he'd fibbed.

"Mind if I have a little fun now that you're pretty sure I'm not going to kill us?" she asked. "We have plenty of extra fuel for this run."

"Does that mean you're going to show me what this thing can really do?" Archer teased. "I wasn't going to point out that you drive like a grandma..."

That might have been the wrong thing to say.

Waverly screeched, then muttered, "I'll show you a granny."

She did a pretty good job of making sure he'd never malign her again with a daring swoop that brought them low over the waves as they circled back. Soon they buzzed Tosin and Miguel.

It got even better when Miguel stumbled at their unexpected nearness, and fell overboard with a splash. They zipped around like a gnat, crisscrossing the air over the guys until they were sure Miguel had climbed in safe and sound—if soaked—once more.

Only when he offered them a double-fingered salute did they fly off again, laughing.

Waverly hadn't finished with her freestyling, though.

She swerved her way from island to island on the general course to their destination. Lush foliage and even a waterfall they spotted along the way made for an amazing tour of the area.

If Archer didn't have a stomach of steel and immunity to motion sickness after years of working on a boat, he might have ruined their afternoon. Instead, he whooped and cheered as she took him for the ride of his life.

Even if he did clutch the seat in a death grip a time or two.

The highlight of the trip came when they passed over a marshy inlet on one of the bigger landmasses. An entire flock of flamingos launched themselves into the air, not high enough to be a concern. Looking down on a sight he'd seen numerous times from the ground in Bonaire gave him a new viewpoint.

Just like Waverly kept doing to him in other aspects of his life.

For one, he hadn't felt so aggressive with her, didn't always need to be in control like he had with other partners. Though, there went his cock again...the thought held some appeal. Maybe someday, after their unfortunate start was further in the shadows of the past, he could ask her to explore the clubroom with him.

For now, playing in the sunlight with her was everything he could hope for.

His restlessness, and most of his bitterness, had vanished, too.

He felt weightless. As if he could fly without the chopper, though he didn't plan to put that to the test.

"Are you sure you gave me the right coordinates?" She glanced at him then, looking a little nervous as she punched buttons on her various monitors. "I don't see any outposts for the supply run."

"Don't worry, Waverly." He smiled. "We're in the right place for what I had in mind. There's a clearing right over there that you can put us down in, if that works for you."

Given that she often landed helicopters on postage-stamp-sized pads that were essentially moving targets, he had figured it would be a cakewalk for her.

The guys had scoped it out for him and taken pictures that he'd reviewed with Captain Alex, who also had an extensive knowledge of aviation from his own time in the Navy. The guy had given Archer the thumbs-up on his selection. Just in case, they had plenty of gas to make it back if she didn't feel comfortable for whatever reason.

"Archer?" she asked. "Is this *really* a business thing we're doing?"

"Nope." He grinned then, knowing the jig was up. "It's a very, very personal thing. A romantic-as-fuck date thing."

"Seriously?" She raised her brows but kept her eyes forward as she descended, landing dead-center in the clearing.

"Yes. This whole helicopter pilot business is awfully convenient. I loved my life before all this, Waverly. I swear I did. But some of these perks..."

"I totally know what you mean." She finished shutting down, hopped from the helicopter, then waited for him near the edge of the palm trees. "I mean, in my old job, I never got to make out with my boss."

They kissed for a while, forgetting where they were or that the rest of the world even existed outside of this slice of heaven. Eventually, he entwined their fingers and led her toward the beach on the south side of the islet.

When the path opened up and he could see what his friends had prepared, he realized why they had taken so damn long. They'd gone overboard for him today. Twice, he thought with a chuckle. Knowing they cared enough to help him score points with Waverly only made the day that much more meaningful.

"Oh, Archer." She dropped her shoes and jogged the rest of the way toward the set up, her hair and dress blowing in the breeze as if she were a sea goddess. He'd never seen someone more elegant and gorgeous than her right then.

He wished he were a painter so that he could capture the moment forever.

When she looked back at him, the undiluted bliss on her face—rosy cheeks, sparkling eyes, and captivating smile—made the mountain of suffering they'd done before finding each other again worth it. If he could spend a day like this with her even every once in a while, he'd die happy.

In the midst of hundreds of currently unlit pillar candles that dotted the beach, she spun around, her arms out.

At their very center was a humongous heart drawn in the sand. Of course his smartass friends hadn't been able to resist and had also written *Archie + Waverly 4Ever*. He felt less guilty about Miguel's impromptu dip after that, though Waverly seemed to love it.

She took out her phone and snapped pictures of the setup from every angle, as if she never wanted to forget a thing about it.

Two upside down, squared off U's constructed of driftwood at least as tall as him had been pounded into the sand and draped with a long panel of sheer fabric, which fluttered in the wind. It provided shelter from the afternoon sun for the blanket spread and staked beneath it. A dozen or more oversized pillows made the space seem comforting and inviting.

Nearby, a table for two was set, and an ice chest waited for them to unpack it.

A handful of tiki torches scattered around completed the masterpiece.

Everything they needed for an exclusive, romantic retreat...they had it.

Most importantly, they had each other.

After the double drama of the day before—their emotional turmoil and the near-mugging, which the local authorities weren't interested in investigating—they could use a day away from the rest of the world.

He planned to give her that.

Hopefully complete with lots of bone-melting sex.

What better way to relax was there than that?

SEVENTEEN

Archer thought for a change of pace he would try drawing things out instead of pouncing on Waverly immediately. Each time they'd fucked the night before he'd had intentions of going slowly, taking her impossibly gently, but never seemed to make it past a few kisses before he lost every shred of restraint he possessed. Just like he had in the hotel in Caracas. Or hell, even the night she'd come to him the first time.

She didn't help his cause, though, when she asked, "We're alone here, right?"

"Completely," he confirmed.

It was only a three syllable word, but by the time he got to the end of it, she'd grabbed the hem of her dress and whisked it over her head. Her bra and panties followed soon after as she made a beeline for the shore.

He started to jog toward her, leaving his own clothes in a trail on the sand as he ran to catch up with her. When he did, he growled, "Damn, you are something."

"Something good, I hope." She peeked up at him, still a tiny bit shy at her very core, giving him a glimpse of the girl he used to know.

"Magnificent." He wrapped his arms around her bare shoulders and drew her to him for a kiss that felt more sensual to him than fucking had with other partners in the past. He savored the coconut and lime flavor of her lip gloss as he attempted to seduce her mouth with his own.

Her hands ran down his sides to his ass, kneading the muscles there even as she attempted to yank him closer to her. He resisted, not wanting to get carried away too soon.

Breaking their kiss, he said, "Come on."

Their fingers automatically found their way to each other again, knitting together as they headed for the surf. It broke gently on the pristine white beach. When they reached it, Waverly kicked, splashing and laughing as if neither of them had a care in the world.

Did they have worries anymore? It didn't seem like it when they were together.

Right now the only thing on his mind was making this a perfect afternoon and evening for her.

For them both.

He led her deeper, first up to their knees and then a little more. His hips were below the surge. Taller than her by a half a foot or so, he was steadier at that depth. So he braced her by putting his arms around her in another tender embrace.

The guys would never let him hear the end of it if he admitted that this—staring into her eyes, laughing together, and simply enjoying life—would be enough to satisfy him. Even if he didn't know they were about to rival the intensity of the sun with their lovemaking, he would have been content just to hold her.

"You know, before you came back into my life, I'd sworn off meaningless affairs," he told her then.

"Whatever." She rolled her eyes. "I saw that woman leaving your cabin less than an hour before we were reintroduced, remember?"

"Yeah, that was a moment of weakness. One that made it clear I was over that kind of hook up." He grinned. "But thanks for making my vow of celibacy a short-lived one."

She laughed.

He tucked a strand of hair behind her ear even though it only blew loose again immediately, wild and free, just like her. "I knew as soon as I saw you again that it hadn't felt right because I wasn't with the right person. I've only barely gotten you back, so this probably sounds crazy, but you've always been the one for me, Waverly. I know that now. It doesn't feel like this with anyone else."

"For me either." She burrowed into his chest before continuing, "I dated. Slept with a handful of guys who were nice enough. Polite enough. Successful enough. But none of them ever made me desperate to be with them, like you do."

"Does it scare you?" he asked.

"A little. After I left home, I swore I'd never depend on anyone again. But I'm starting to feel like if I don't have you, I can't be happy now that I see what it's like already and the potential for what we could become to each other. It's hard to give up control of my own destiny like that. And I have a feeling it's only going to get more intense."

He nodded, understanding perfectly. "Then at least I have company. I'm terrified, Waverly. Of fucking this up, of not deserving you, of not being able to be what you need."

Silently, he thought of the clubroom on the *Divemaster* and what it would be like to tuck that facet of his sexuality away for good. It wasn't as if Waverly was a submissive woman. He would miss it, but he thought he could make compromises, if it meant keeping her in his bed.

And his life.

"Don't worry, Archer. You tick all my boxes. Everything I've ever wanted—everything I looked for in a man—was someone like you." As she said it, she hopped, wrapping her legs around his hips.

He caught her, groaning as the heat of her pussy seared his bobbing erection, which had been chilled by the sea a moment earlier. "I'm falling for you, Waverly. All over again. Twice as hard, for this new and improved version of you."

Her tight little nipples scored his chest as she rubbed against him.

"I've been obsessed with you since I was sixteen. I don't see that changing any time soon. Especially not if you keep rocking my world in bed...or on the beach. It's better every time. More than I could have imagined possible."

Neither one of them dropped the L-word. He was okay with that. It was too quick for her to really mean it, considering how wary they'd both been forced to become about their surroundings and the people closest to them. When she said it to him, he wanted to believe it completely.

He'd work on earning it. Forever if he had to.

Starting right then.

When she was ready to hear it from him, he was prepared to say it.

"I can't give you back your first time—*our* first time. But I can try to make every time even more special than the last." Archer palmed her ass, making her squirm. The motion only aligned them better, his cock nudging her pussy. He kissed her again then, spending an inordinate amount of time exploring the textures and tastes of her mouth with his tongue, teeth, and lips.

When neither of them could stand to be teased any longer—by the warm water washing over them, the heat they generated, or the intimacy of the moment—he carried her up onto the beach.

He didn't go far.

Couldn't, honestly.

So he sank to his knees right where the waves kissed the shore and laid her out before him. Her spread hair floated and moved each time the water came up to swirl lightly around them, making her look like a siren. Especially as she beckoned him nearer by spreading her legs.

When she cupped her own breasts as she stared up at him stroking himself a few times to the sight of her, he buckled.

Archer leaned down and took her nipple into his mouth, lapping and tugging until she cried out his name. He left it with a kiss then did the same to her other side, balancing his attentions. Meanwhile, his hand traveled along her softly rounded stomach to her mound and began to rub gentle circles around her clit as he devoured her breasts.

"Please, Archer. Fuck me," she begged when she finally cracked.

His cock pulsed at the thought of her welcoming heat and slickness. But no, not yet.

"Not until you've come on my face a few times. Feed me your pleasure, Waverly. I want to learn what it tastes like. Get my fill so I can never forget." He slithered down her body until he could blow lightly over her pussy.

She moaned and arched as if she might come from that alone.

He sank a couple fingers into her, loving the way she hugged him tight, just before he applied his open mouth to her outer lips. He let her adjust before easing closer to her center. When his tongue licked her clit for the first time, she shattered, surprising them both.

Waverly's orgasms were sweet.

To watch, and to taste. He wanted more of them.

To be the cause of them.

Archer eased up until she'd recovered, then started the process over again, bringing her up and letting her crest a few times. His cock leaked, dripping pearly fluid into the water where it swirled before disappearing into the ocean.

But he still didn't take her or the release her body would so easily grant him. Not yet.

He gathered Waverly into his arms and stood when he noticed she shivered slightly. In the sun, blanketed by his full form, she'd warm right up.

She curled into him, utterly relaxed, trusting, and docile as he transported her to their makeshift cabana. Her complete surrender transfixed him. The strongest woman he had ever known was putting herself in his hands. It made him wonder if someday she might be up for testing deeper waters with him after all.

Was this her true self? The one at the core of the tough-talking, fiercely independent warrior he adored? If so, he knew he had to be delicate with her now because she wouldn't often expose this vulnerable part of herself.

Archer deposited her as gently as possible on the soft blanket and propped her hips up with a pillow. He wanted this to be perfect for her.

"Please, Archer." She drew his attention to her wide eyes, which blinked slowly up at him despite the sunshine illuminating the world around them. "I need you."

"I need you, too." He'd never spoken a truer vow than that.

Except he wasn't only talking about her body.

He needed all of her. For keeps.

It seemed only a fair exchange since he'd given her all of himself and never wanted it back.

Surrendering to primal desire, Archer gathered her wrists in one hand and pinned them to the blanket. The force of his hold made a divot in the sand below, helping him keep her securely in place. With the other, he strangled the bottom of his shaft, certain he'd never been this hard in his entire life before.

There was nothing left to say. Instead, he stared into her eyes, which were a reflection of the bluest skies and the deepest oceans, as he fed her his cock inch by inch.

Agonizingly slowly, he penetrated her, giving her everything he had.

And when they'd locked together, as tightly fused as possible, he began to move.

With subtle rocks of his hips, he pressed into her again and again, never retreating very far. It was a whole new kind of fucking for him but it felt right, so he kept doing it. Slow, steady, rhythmic pressure. Whatever it was, it seemed to be working.

Waverly's eyes had turned glassy and dazed as she took what he gave her and loved every second.

Her channel clenched around him, threatening to milk him dry far too soon.

He bent down to kiss her, craving connection at every possible pleasure point.

And when he slipped his tongue into her mouth, she screamed, vocalizing her climax. How he didn't break then and pour himself inside her, he didn't know.

He could tell she had more left in her.

Stopping before she was fully satisfied wasn't an option.

Archer sat up a little, kneeling between her legs to gain leverage so he could fuck the old-fashioned way.

They both groaned as he took those first ultra-deep lunges within her.

Soon he was sliding his cock in her as far as he could reach, then withdrawing until he would have slipped free if it wasn't for the perfectly timed flex of her muscles, which locked around the head of his cock and held him within her. His balls got in on the action, slapping up against her ass when he really dug in.

The soft impact was another stimulant. There were too many to resist now. It wasn't a matter of if he was going to come, but when.

Waverly made the decision for him when, on a particularly vigorous thrust, she rose up. Strung tight, she shattered. She yelled out his name over and over, begging him to join her in rapture.

It was an unnecessary request. A blaze of pleasure at the base of his cock was followed by the pumping of every bit of his come directly from his balls into her pussy. He came so hard and so long that he overflowed her.

Waverly levered up onto her elbows to watch the spot where they were joined. Both of them witnessed his seed spilling out of her and trickling toward her ass.

The sight had him mesmerized.

He hoped she realized that with this act, he'd staked a claim, one he never intended to forgo.

Waverly crashed then, a slave to her ecstasy and the endorphins pumping through her bloodstream. So he tended to her, using some of the washcloths and supplies the guys had left on the sidelines to clean her up and make her comfortable.

He adjusted the material covering their shelter to make sure she was shaded properly, got her a bottle of ice water to sip, and brought her a few chocolate-covered strawberries to snack on.

Only then did he settle in beside her, giving her the last thing she required.

Him.

It amazed Archer that he could be part of that equation.

Neither of them interrupted the rush of the waves in the background or the call of the birds in the trees behind them with unnecessary words. They'd said everything before they'd come together.

Archer couldn't believe how satisfied he was. All this time, he'd been doing it wrong.

As he'd suspected, sex with someone who meant more than a good time or simple relief was next level shit. Nothing else would do ever again.

Eventually, he dozed, still wrapped around Waverly, protecting her as best he could even while unconscious.

When he woke, the sun rode low on the horizon. Waverly had already gotten up and was putting the finishing touches on their picnic dinner. Okay, so that was the understatement of the century. It was a fancy-ass meal that he was sure to enjoy because it had been prepared for them by people who cared, and would be shared with the love of his life.

Shhh, he thought, afraid to even think it in case she could read his mind. She wasn't ready to hear it yet, but that didn't make it any less true. He stretched, then realized the sand looked like it was moving.

He scrubbed his eyes and looked again.

She'd been busy, lighting the candles. The flames danced all over the beach.

When the sun fell below the horizon, it was going to be gorgeous.

A little while later, they were humming and sighing over the delicacies they devoured when Waverly said, "So that whole indigenous people aid story…"

"Actually, that was true." He smiled. "But we didn't want to freak them out by sending the chopper the first time we made contact. Tosin and Miguel brought the stuff over by boat. When we saw them earlier, they were coming back from the run. They also gave the locals a head's up that we would be dropping by the neighborhood so that they didn't think we were stranded over here. Wouldn't want anyone to barge in looking for survivors in need of help."

"Good thinking." She winked at him. "Because I wasn't about to stop, no matter who came wandering by."

"Seriously?" His cock perked up at the thought, surprising even him. Damn, he thought he'd be good until they climbed into their bed tonight at least. But riding a woman while his friends watched, witnessing what he was capable of doing for his partner, was actually one of his favorite lecherous activities.

"Hell yeah." She laughed. "For a show like that, we could probably have charged admission."

He knew she was teasing. Still, he found himself adoring her just a tiny bit more. He held his hand out to her and she took it.

Archer kissed the back of her fingers.

"You've still got it, you know," she said breathily. "That Prince Charming thing. It's in there somewhere, way down deep."

"Do you like that?" he wondered. "I enjoyed life as a simple man, but maybe there's a middle ground."

"I do. I like all the parts of you, Archer."

"Good, because I'm thinking I'd like to eat my dessert off of you before showing you just how much my parts like you back." So much for waiting until later.

He grabbed their chocolate cake and barked, "Strip."

"Yes, sir."

He shuddered.

They didn't have a lot of time left here, and when she artlessly said things like that, she mashed his buttons. While she obliged his command, he did the same.

"Well, hello. There's my sexy swordfish," she sing-songed as she blatantly stared at his erection.

Archer choked. "Never let Miguel and Tosin hear you say that. *Please*."

She flopped to her back in their nest of cushions and laughed as loud as she pleased, knowing he was the only one around to witness her amusement and total abandon. It didn't take long, though, before neither of them was giggling.

Grunts and moans filled the evening when he placed her on her hands and knees in front of him. She lowered her face to the blanket and put her ass up, with her arms folded above her head. She was the picture of perfection.

Archer fucked her then, more savagely than he intended.

Her breasts swayed as he clamped his hands on her hips and used his grip to impale her on his stiff shaft. She didn't seem to mind, coming all over his cock just before he pulled out and decorated her ass with shot after shot of his seed.

After a quick dip to clean off, they finished feeding each other their dessert with fingers coated in chocolate.

As daylight faded into night, and the candles illuminated their sanctuary, he leaned over to his pile of clothes to check his watch again. Only a few more minutes to go…

"Got a hot date or something?" Waverly asked when she caught him, though she flashed him a wicked grin when she said it.

"As a matter of fact, I do." He tugged her into his lap, spellbound by how perfect she felt in his arms, curled against his body. Like it was where she belonged. Because it was.

And then, there in the brilliant sunset, a familiar ship was silhouetted.

"It's the *Divemaster*!" Waverly actually clapped.

"Yeah, Miguel and Tosin have one more surprise for you."

She buried her face in his neck for a second, though he wished she would have stayed that way longer. "Oh, man. I feel really bad about my stunts this morning."

"I wouldn't. It's not going to be long before they're pulling some prank on you. They're just giving you a head start."

"I'm glad we'll have a really short flight back." Waverly kissed him then.

"Yeah, I didn't want you to have to fly in the dark after a whole day of exhausting ourselves on this excursion."

"I meant because I might not make it through another flight where you're sporting wood within reach. Two of my favorite things at once. It's overload." She sighed. "You're not the only one who gets riled up on those trips."

"I would normally say it's not going to be a problem, after a day like this, but with you...I can't help myself." He grinned.

"Only fair since it seems like the more I have of you, the more I want," she whispered.

"I'm not going to complain about that."

She sighed. "Thank you for today, Archer. For everything."

They kissed then, with heat and promise. His hand cupped the side of her neck.

In the background, the sky turned gold and red as fireworks exploded then trickled down toward the ocean. Waverly paused and glanced out to sea without breaking their connection.

They made out as the show continued, the explosions of light and sound complementing the impact they had on each other.

∽ EIGHTEEN ∽

A week and a half or so later, Waverly reclined on an obscenely comfortable lounge chair. It was strategically positioned near the railing on a lower deck so she could see Archer doing his thing down below.

The damn chaise kept tempting her to drift off into a nap to make up for some of the rest she'd happily sacrificed while "sleeping" with Archer instead. That probably wouldn't be recommended for a few reasons.

First, because the skimpy bikini she had worn to drive Archer nuts left a whole lot of her exposed, and sunscreen only cut it for so long. Risking a massive burn on her ass or thighs or boobs or any of Archer's other favorite places to manhandle might keep her sidelined from rasping against the sheets as he made love to her. No thanks.

That was a risk she wasn't willing to take.

More importantly, though, she'd chosen this spot to work on her tan so she could keep her eye on her man, who was doing who-knew-what as he puttered around on the dive deck. Whatever it was, it seemed to be satisfying him. He smiled often, whistling while he worked.

It was gratifying to see him embracing his new life.

One that miraculously included her.

Together, they were living the *Divemaster* dream.

Rather than risk falling asleep, she decided to wander down there for a close-up view of the action. As she did, she looked around at their surroundings. They hadn't seen another boat in forever. Wherever they were, it felt really remote.

Waverly wouldn't have minded if they never went back to the real world.

"Hey there, can I help you, miss?" Archer came up behind her, kissing her neck as he looped his arms around her waist.

She leaned into his touch. "Just came to say hi. I missed you."

"I agree. It's been far too long since we've been together." He groaned, rubbing his semi on her ass.

Waverly laughed. "It's been less than an hour. You're insatiable."

"When it comes to you? Yes, I am." He squeezed her and they stood together, admiring the view.

"Where are we anyway?" she asked.

"It's kind of dumb. Don't laugh. We got hired to work this charter once and ended up diving somewhere in this vicinity. We were on our way back in and Miguel *swore* he saw something down in the sand."

"What did you see?" Waverly turned to the other guy, who was sitting nearby, and asked him directly.

"I don't give a fuck if they want to harass me for it." He crossed his arms, making her think he wasn't being exactly honest about that. "I saw jewels. Treasure. I'm sure of it."

She leaned forward, imagining how it would sparkle under the water while fish swam lazily above it. "So why didn't you investigate?"

"We'd been diving a lot on that trip. It was my fifth one of the day and I was going to require decompression if I went back down." He cursed in Spanish.

Archer grimaced then. "What he's being too nice to say is that I talked him out of making it an issue with the captain."

"*We* did," Tosin sighed. "We figured there'd be plenty of time to poke around on our dives the next day."

"Except that night a huge storm took a freak twist and headed straight for us. We had to pull up anchor and dodge the weather." Miguel groaned as if it still pained him. "The charter had no choice but to go back into port. On our next day off, we took a prop plane flight as close as we could get, rented a boat, and checked it out. Though we have a pretty good idea of where we were, it was impossible to tell *precisely* where we'd been anchored. The sand in the area had been totally redistributed by the storm, erasing some landmarks we'd used. Hell, maybe it's something about the topography there that causes those freak cells to strike. That could explain what doomed the ship in the first place."

The way he talked about it wasn't like the sunken treasure was a possibility. It was a certainty.

Miguel believed it.

And they believed him.

Waverly felt a tiny pang of jealousy over their bond, except she realized that their friendship extended to her through Archer.

"We haven't told anyone. Nobody except the three of us knows about this," Archer said, giving her some warm tingly goodness. They trusted her, too.

"Now's the perfect chance to poke around a little. Maybe the sand has shifted again. We could get lucky." Miguel seemed even more eager than usual to get in the water.

"Not that we need the money anymore, but...who doesn't want to find a long-lost pirate's booty?" Tosin's eyes probably gleamed as much as the jewels they hoped to find.

"So you're going down to look for it. Cool. Can I come?" she asked. She didn't dive as often as they did. Still, she loved joining Archer in the place he loved so much on occasion. Even without the possibility of riches, she would enjoy her time with them.

"I was hoping you'd want to." He held her tighter, hugging her to his chest. In her ear he whispered, "Maybe someday you'll help me live out *my* underwater fantasies."

Unlike Miguel's, she figured his involved sex. How would that work exactly?

Determined to find out, she waited until Archer had gone to retrieve her gear from their private locker on the other side of the dive deck.

"Psst. Hey, Miguel, can I ask you something?" She blushed.

"I don't fool around with my friends' girls, but thanks." He grinned, obviously picking up on her naughty vibe.

She smacked him on the ass, hard.

"Damn, babe." He rubbed his butt. "You ever hear the phrase 'swing like a girl'?"

"Hard, you mean?" She dared him to say something stupid then.

"Right. So, anyway…"

She leaned in and whispered so none of the guests lounging around could overhear. "Is it possible to do it underwater?"

"Your man is seriously the luckiest son of a bitch in the universe." Miguel pretended to pout.

She was afraid Archer would finish whatever he was doing and she'd lose her chance to mine information. "Come on, tell me. Maybe nothing too crazy the first time we try it. But, like, what are the odds that Archer's going to drown if I give him a hand job during our safety stop?"

Manslaughtering your boyfriend during sex would probably be traumatizing, she figured.

"I should tell you it's too dangerous, just to fuck with him. But…yeah, go for it. He can handle it." Miguel chuckled. "You've only got one obstacle to a stealth jerk that I can see."

"What?" She hoped she didn't sound too disappointed.

"Wetsuit." He pointed to where his was pulled up his legs and bunched around his waist. unzipped on the top. "Sure, he can doff his BCD and tank and all that shit underwater but it's not really fun. Let me see if I can talk him out of wearing it. Sometimes on our days off we like to dive bare. Skin on ocean. Feels different to have the water pressing all along your body with nothing in between."

Whoa. Miguel really loved the ocean. He talked about it like he would a lover. Sort of like Archer had when they'd decided not to use condoms. She must have looked at him oddly then as she suppressed the urge to blurt *that's what she said.*

He wagged his finger at her. "I didn't even mean it like that. Anyway, it's warm enough here, and we're not going that deep. He doesn't need it."

Then he rummaged in the weight bins, selecting a pair of two pounders. "I'll add these to your back pockets for this dive so you don't have to worry about your buoyancy if you're thrashing around down there. Just remember you'll probably add additional air at depth with these along for the ride, so make sure you let it out on the way up. More than you usually would, okay?"

She nodded. No problem.

"And once you've got him...distracted, it's probably best if you keep an eye on his regulator. If it slips out of his mouth while he's, um, in the middle of something, you might want to grab it and hand it back. He can do a reg retrieve in his sleep, but I'm not sure he's ever tried while he's busting a nut before."

What had she gotten herself into? Waverly put her hand on her flaming face. "Okay, thanks for the advice."

They both laughed kind of awkwardly.

"You're good for him, Waverly," Miguel said as he finished prepping his own stuff. "Good thing, since he'll probably ask you to marry him as soon as you hit the surface."

Her tummy did flip-flops, even though she knew he was joking.

It was way too soon for her to be having thoughts like that about Archer. That didn't mean she wasn't, though.

"Almost ready?" Archer called to them as he finished hooking up her tank and setting out her mask, fins, and snorkel.

Waverly hoped she didn't give away too much with her wicked smile. "Oh, yeah. I'm ready."

Miguel shimmied out of his wetsuit, looking mighty fine as he did. Damn, the man had a lot of muscles. "It's nice out. I'm going without this today."

"Sounds like a plan." Tosin followed his lead, ditching his wetsuit as well.

"Want to try it?" Archer asked her. "It's kind of fun. You don't get cold easily, do you?"

"Never when I'm with you," she sealed the deal.

Waverly did a covert happy dance when Archer bent to tug his wetsuit down his legs while Miguel hid a laugh behind a faux cough.

❧ NINETEEN ❧

Waverly held Archer's hand as they stepped off the back of the *Divemaster* and took a plunge into the unknown. She wasn't nervous going down. Not with him by her side.

No matter what they found, or didn't, they'd handle it together.

The first thing she realized about bikini-only SCUBA was that the giant stride was positively wedgie-inducing. Miguel looked over at her with laughter in his eyes as she plucked the fabric out of her crack. She figured that was payback for the helicopter stunt the other day, so she gave him a quasi-friendly finger.

He wrote something on his slate then turned it so she could see. A giant smiley face with HA HA HA coming out of its mouth. Tosin snagged it out of his hand, added "x 2", then showed it to her again. She peeked over at Archer only to find him struggling not to laugh. So she shoved his shoulder. He took her hand, brought it toward him, and slipped his regulator out of his mouth long enough to kiss her knuckles before putting it back in.

If she had been out in the atmosphere, she would have sighed.

He presented a thumbs-down and she nodded.

When they'd descended forty-seven feet to the bottom of the shallow shelf not far from the *Divemaster*, Miguel, Tosin, and Archer began flashing each other hand gestures that made absolutely no sense to her. It was fascinating to watch how they communicated, working together seamlessly.

After about thirty seconds, Miguel and Tosin peeled off and headed over a ridge. They swam as fluidly as the fish around them. She started to follow. Archer squeezed her hand and shook his head. He pressed his fingers and the thumb of his right hand together until it formed a flat blade. Then—arm extended—he gestured with it, in the opposite direction.

Oh. They were splitting up into pairs to cover more ground.

Made sense.

Plus, Miguel might have been doing her a favor, granting them some privacy and giving them the easier assignment so they could fool around without undue risk. She was shocked at how close to the surface the reef was here, and how it seemed to slope upward as it got farther out to sea. In some places, it seemed like it might poke through the waves into the air depending on the tide.

If there really was a shipwreck somewhere around here, she wouldn't be surprised. That would be a bitch to run up on unexpectedly, especially in bad weather like the guys had described.

Ordinarily, or at least on other dives she'd done with Archer lately, they crept along, investigating the reef in a direct path. Today he did something different. Something she recognized after a moment or two. He pointed to an unusually large sea fan.

She thought it was beautiful, too, with its lacey panels.

Until she realized he wasn't sightseeing. He was using it as a marker. Of where they started. Then they spiraled outward in a standard search pattern, making sure not to overlap or leave gaps in their trail. He used a compass and took a lot of notes on his slate to keep track of where they'd been. When something unusual caught his eye, he aimed a torch at it, though none of the leads turned out to be anything other than the usual rocks covered with algae or coral.

Unlike other times, they didn't dally. Instead, they swam at a pretty steady clip while they scanned back and forth. They didn't follow the reef at all, focusing on the sandy patches in between the coral mounds more heavily.

After forty-five minutes, she wondered if Miguel and Tosin were having any better luck. She hadn't seen anything except the pristine natural beauty one would expect this far from the normal tourist destinations. She eyed her dive watch to check their bottom time, then peeked at her air gauge. Although she had more than nine hundred pounds remaining, she shook the little metal cylinder Archer had hooked to her BCD with a carabiner earlier.

A ball bearing rattled around inside, making a distinct noise—similar to a ringing bell—that got his attention in a hurry.

He whipped his head around to face her.

His eyes locked on hers through their masks as if asking, *What's wrong?*

Even from there, their coffee color distracted her with their richness. He shrugged at her.

Oh. Oops. She pointed to her air gauge and then to the line that led from the ship's anchor upward. Good thing she'd only planned to attempt a hand job. She'd have to wait until they visited someplace with a shore entry and a shallow, beach-y stretch to execute any more complicated maneuvers.

Hanging on the line during their safety stop would mean she only had one hand available.

Still, she felt comfortable enough to move ahead to stage two of her wicked plan.

Side-by-side, they ascended. She made sure to dump all the air from her BCD like Miguel had instructed her. She noticed the pull of the extra weights, but it wasn't difficult to kick lightly toward the surface to counteract them. They'd come in handy if she got distracted in a minute.

It was easier to swim up than it was to slow your ascent if you got out of control.

Waverly had no desire to experience the bends. That would probably ruin Archer's good time, too. After everything he'd done for her—from saving her life, to giving her a dream job, to providing a place to live on the *Divemaster*, to the grand romantic gesture of their beach date, and all the everyday things he did to show her that he cared—she wanted to do this for him.

Show time.

Archer grabbed hold of the line when they were exactly fifteen feet deep. She hoped they weren't clearly visible to the people on the *Divemaster*. Because right then she made her move.

Instead of gripping the rope beside his hand, she put her palms on his shoulders and clung to him. His eyes sparkled with joy, even through his mask. When he took his regulator out, she did the same, remembering to blow tiny bubbles the entire time it wasn't in her mouth as she'd been trained.

Quickly, they came together, sharing a brief but powerful kiss.

Then he was nudging her hand, putting her regulator between her lips and tapping the button on the front to clear the water from it. Smart, since the maneuver had definitely stolen some of her concentration and all of her breath.

He pointed to the rope, indicating she should hang on.

She glanced at her dive computer, steadily ticking off the 170 seconds to go before they could surface safely. So she shook her head no and scooted her hands down his torso, until her face was level with his crotch. Using his hips as her handholds she was steady, only kicking every once in a while as the extra weight Miguel had added to her BCD did its job, keeping her under.

Waverly peeked up at Archer, who had gone stock-still.

He was staring at her.

So she didn't disappoint. She shoved his suit down to the tops of his thighs, just low enough to expose his cock. It was half-hard by the time she wrapped her fingers around it and began to pump. He made a gurgling noise, so she looked up to make sure he was okay.

Oh, he was fine.

Looking like an ancient god of the sea as he hovered above her, he leveled a commanding glare at her. In her mind, she could imagine him growling, "Don't stop."

So she didn't.

Waverly ran her fingers up and down his length, cupping his balls every once in a while. When his hips began to rock, thrusting his hard-on through the ring of her fingers, she knew he was enjoying himself. Dangling off the anchor line, submerged in the ocean he loved so much, he took the pleasure she gave him.

Both of them knew it wouldn't last long.

She pumped harder, as fast as she could given the resistance of the water.

His breathing became erratic, sending gushes of bubbles to the surface. Quickly, she peeked at his air gauge. Insanely efficient with his breathing most times, he still had five-hundred pounds more than she did. He'd be fine even if he sucked down some extra puffs.

Waverly began to tease him then, sliding the pad of her thumb across the underside of his shaft and onto the head as she added a twist of her wrist to her jacking. Muscles rippled along the entire length of his body as he gave himself fully to the experience.

A few seconds more and his free hand squeezed her shoulder. She understood what he was trying to tell her. He was about to come. So she took a deep breath, popped her regulator out, then finished him off. With her mouth.

It was an odd sensation. Though she fit her lips around the tip of his shaft before sliding down it, a trickle of salty water got in her mouth along with the release he pumped down her throat immediately upon her first contact. He came so hard, she couldn't quite get it all before she had to pull off and reclaim her air source.

She cleared her regulator, coughing a few times as she got settled. Archer watched her the whole time, making sure she was safe.

In the meantime, she examined him as he wrapped his hand around his cock and stroked himself through the remainder of his orgasm. Silky strands of his come rippled in the current like ribbons as they floated away.

Waverly double-checked to make sure he was breathing okay when his chest expanded with an enormous breath followed by an equally huge exhalation. His regulator was still in place. Check and check.

Then his entire body sagged, deadweight on the end of his arm. His hand still instinctively clung to the rope.

That's when she noticed the look in his eyes. It was nearly enough to make her spontaneously combust, if by combust you meant come on the spot. He reached for her then, with the hand not still clutching the line for dear life.

So she swam up to him.

Again, they shared a brief underwater kiss. She thought they'd have to practice this skill a lot more often. It made her feel like he was the center of her universe. Because in that moment, he was.

When he motioned for her to put her regulator back in one last time, his bonelessness evaporated with a jerk. Then his eyes got *humongous.*

What? Was Jaws about to make a meal out of her?

She whipped around, but there was nothing behind her.

When she looked back she realized it wasn't her he'd been gawking at. He must have felt something slipping. Because now, as they dangled there on the rope together, she followed his stare far below their flippers to where his bathing suit was sinking into oblivion.

Now *that* was funny!

Waverly laughed so hard she choked a little. He was right there, making sure she was okay. She pointed at her dive computer, which said their safety stop was complete. Time to get out.

He shook his head no vigorously, then gestured to his junk.

She shrugged. It wasn't like he had anything to be embarrassed about. He was hung.

Archer rubbed his forehead, looked down again wistfully in the direction of his long-gone trunks, then released a huge cloud of bubbles she could only assume was an exasperated sigh.

He gave her a thumbs-up.

They slowly ascended the rest of the way to the surface.

Waverly was surprised to see Miguel and Tosin on the dive platform. How had they made it out so quickly? Sure, they'd gone deeper than her and Archer, which meant they couldn't stay under as long, but they were practically marine mammals and could make their air last forever. Whereas she'd called their dive early so she could fool around.

Of course, Archer did not take this as good news. She heard him mutter, "Fuck."

A laugh escaped her.

Miguel must have heard. He looked down at them. "Getting out?"

"Could someone toss me a towel?" Archer asked.

"It's traditional to use those once you've left the ocean. They're not very effective for drying off if you get them soaked," the other guy teased, but he looked to Waverly as if asking how things had gone. She winked then headed for the ladder.

"Waverly!" Archer begged.

"Remember when you laughed at my unfortunate wedgie incident? Toodle-oo." She gave him a finger wave over her shoulder then hauled herself and her bazillion pounds of equipment onto the ship.

Tosin joined them, peering overboard. "What's taking so long? Hustle, would you? We have something to show you."

Waverly couldn't help but turn around and stare when the two divemasters began to crack up. Whistles and catcalls cut through the afternoon, drawing the attention of the guests. Even Captain Alex, who must have been making rounds.

The captain surprised everyone when he called Archer out on the tan lines left by the tiny triangle his suit usually covered. From a few decks above them it was easy to hear him shout, "Put some pants on, kid. You're blinding us up here."

Archer shuffled across the dive deck, his fins held in front of him to preserve some of his modesty. A shame, really.

By the time she made her way to her slot at the bench, dropped her tank in the holder, and got her gear off, Archer was back. He wore a pair of cotton shorts that he usually pulled on over his swim trunks. They rode low on his hips, showing off his washboard abs and the V that pointed straight to her favorite new toy. He flipped off Miguel and Tosin as he came to help her break down her set-up.

"Not pissed?" she asked as she chuckled.

"After what you did down there, it would take a hell of a lot more than that to put me in a bad mood." He leaned in and kissed her solidly, making her hope they were headed back to their cabin for a mid-afternoon quickie. "That was fucking incredible. Thank you."

"Maybe next time we can swap places." She thought of the possibilities and hummed.

"Archie!" Miguel called from the table in the center of the dive deck. "You two can bask in the afterglow later. Get over here already."

He held his hand out to her and she took it. Together they approached the other two divemasters.

"What the hell is so important?" Archer glared at them. "I was thinking I might need to be kind of busy for the next hour or two or ten."

"Well, my friend." Tosin positively beamed. "I may not have joined the Going Down club today, but I think this makes a nice consolation prize."

He lifted the edge of the towel on the table to give them a peek at what was beneath.

It was blood red, the size of a golf ball.

"It coordinates well with this, I think." Miguel was grinning then too as he revealed the fistfuls of gold coins he'd retrieved.

Holy shit.

They'd found it.

"It was right where I remembered." Miguel hummed. "Just waiting for us to come back and do this right. Now we actually have the resources to retrieve what's down there. Maybe sometimes things really do happen for a reason."

Archer whooped. He tugged Waverly into his arms and spun her around. The whole time, he stared into her eyes. "You know, I think they're right about that."

"So do I."

～ TWENTY ～

Later that night Archer sat in a private nook on one of the upper decks with Tosin, Miguel, and Banks. They huddled around a table with tons of documents scattered across it. Who could have known it would require this much paperwork to set his plans in motion?

A bunch of empty beer bottles made perfect paperweights, warding off the breezes that kept getting stronger the longer they hung out. He did his part to help by draining another one then plunking it on top of the contract he'd just signed.

Away from city lights, the night sky sparkled as if it were littered with the diamonds they hoped to find when they could explore the shipwreck further. They'd spent the afternoon taking pictures and documenting the exact coordinates of the visible portions. Then they'd agreed it was best to take off, heading back to Bonaire for the end of their guests' stay.

The last thing they wanted to do was tip anyone off about what was waiting beneath the waves. If they weren't careful, treasure hunters would swarm the site, compromising the integrity of the find and cherry-picking valuable items.

They would have to keep the secret safe for the few weeks it would take to have the Banks Foundation file a claim, get any necessary permits, and organize an official salvage operation as one of its divisions. Now that most of their business was wrapped up, Archer couldn't wait for Waverly to finish the massage he'd convinced her to get so that he could talk to the guys alone about their future.

Five more minutes, then he'd go search her out.

"I have one last thing I want to ask you all." Archer scanned the face of each man around the table. "We're joint owners here, so I don't have the authority to give our shit away, but with my portion of the treasure proceeds, I'd like to buy our helicopter from the Divemaster Project."

It wasn't too hard to figure out what he might intend to do with one of those.

"Wow, that's a hell of a Valentine's Day gift. Are you in loooooove, Archie?" Tosin teased him as he had known the guy wouldn't be able to resist doing.

"I—" Of course he loved Waverly. Loving someone and being in love with them were two different things, though. And he hadn't said those words out loud to anyone yet. Not even himself.

Banks smiled at him.

"Yeah. Have been since I was eighteen, I think." He rubbed the back of his neck. "Here's the thing. The same way I didn't want you guys to feel stuck here, I'm having the same issue with her."

"She doesn't like working for her boyfriend?" Miguel asked. "I guess I can understand that."

"Waverly doesn't have a problem with it so much as I do." He cleared his throat. "I was hoping I could give her the helicopter, then we could hire her as an independent company to run it. Fair market value on the contract."

"You know, she could decide to take off." Miguel pointed out the obvious. It didn't make Archer's leg stop jittering, either.

"Uh huh. But I'm hoping she won't." He shrugged.

Banks came to his rescue. "I'd say that's a safe bet, Archie."

"I haven't said anything to her about it yet. So can we keep it on the down low until I find the right time?" He rubbed his hand over his mouth and chin. "She can be kind of stubborn about stuff like that sometimes."

The guys laughed at his understatement.

"You know we're happy for you, seriously." Tosin slammed the rest of his beer, then said, "I just want you to be sure, Archer. This is a lot all at once. Our lives have completely changed and—"

"Thanks, but I'm positive."

"If it's the real thing, taking some more time to think things over isn't going to change the outcome," Miguel added.

Archer found himself grinding his teeth. He knew they meant well, but, what the hell? "She's the perfect woman for me. The perfect *partner*. In every way."

Okay, so that might have been a low blow. Both Miguel and Tosin winced.

Could they be jealous of Waverly and the extraordinary amount time he'd been spending with her lately?

"Boys, let it go for tonight," Banks advised them. "Or someone's going to end up with a black eye, and I'm fairly sure the doctor has already turned in for the night. Would hate to wake her up for an ice pack and some x-rays."

"Is someone hurt?" Waverly asked then, making each of them jump. Even Banks.

Whew, that had been close.

In the background, Banks gathered the heap of paperwork and tucked it into an accordion folder that he placed discreetly beside his seat.

"No, Banks is just busting our balls," Miguel answered for them.

"I don't recommend that. I hear it's painful." Waverly smiled as she strolled to Archer and kissed him on the cheek. "Miss me?"

"Tons," he admitted.

If the guys rolled their eyes, he chose to ignore it.

"You were right. That was heavenly. Vanessa is amazing with her hands." Waverly sighed. "I didn't realize how sore I was."

If it wasn't so dark out, he probably could have seen her blush. It wasn't any secret that he'd contributed to her aches by using her so well, so often, lately. Hell, he could have benefited from a rubdown himself. It was a lot of work pleasing her. And he enjoyed every minute of it.

Archer grabbed her around the waist and tugged her into his lap.

"Oh, nice." She squirmed, getting comfortable and putting him in danger of popping a boner at the same time. That's what he got for enjoying her mild embarrassment. "My favorite seat in the house."

"Be careful or he'll put you over those knees next time you're in the clubroom. Bet you won't like that as much," Miguel teased her.

"Huh? What's the clubroom?" she asked, chuckling kind of uncomfortably as if she'd missed the punch line.

Oh, shit.

When she finally noticed the serious stares on the guys' faces, she realized—for once—they weren't joking. "Guys? What'd I miss?"

Miguel clammed up. He looked to Archer as if asking for help out of whatever hole he'd managed to dig for them both. Even Banks raised his brows, which was about as shocked as Archer had ever seen the guy before. Was it that big of a deal that he hadn't felt the need to play in there with her?

Well...maybe.

"Archer?" She looked at him then.

"You've seriously never taken her there?" Tosin asked, making the whole thing worse. "What's up with that? And your little speech earlier... It made it sound like she met *all* your needs. Are you sure, Archie?"

How dare they imply he was changing who he was to suit her? It just hadn't come up yet. Plus, they'd had a lot to work through, given their past. Could *that* be why he had toned down that side of himself around her? Because he still felt guilty? Or like he had to hide those parts of himself?

Could the guys be right?

Damn it. He'd rather believe they were butthurt because he hadn't participated in any late-night private parties, taking that aspect of their bond with him.

"Archer?" Waverly's pitch went up and her volume increased as she repeated herself. She sprang up from his lap and propped her hand on her hip.

They might have had to excuse themselves then to have a very private discussion, and maybe their first serious fight since getting back together, except right then someone screamed.

The animalistic sound left no doubt that something was fucked to hell.

Archer and the rest of the guys shot to their feet, trying to figure out where the noise had come from. A few seconds later, a more controlled shout followed. It didn't ease his anxiety in the least.

"Help! Someone please, help! Oh God, I think she's dead!"

❧ TWENTY-ONE ❧

Archer sprinted toward the hysterical guest, who begged for help.

By the time he arrived, a few other crewmembers and guests had gathered around. The head stewardess, Maria, a married couple from Denver, and one of the ship's officers—Ted—were alternating between trying to calm the screaming person and staring at the pool.

Floating on the surface, face down, in a spreading maroon cloud, was the ship's masseuse.

He skidded to a stop and tried to prevent Waverly from seeing the woman once he realized who it was.

Miguel didn't bother. Though it was unlikely they could help the woman, he dove into the pool and checked for a pulse. He shook his head. No.

When he lifted her face out of the water, he grimaced then set her down gently before heading for the edge. He drew himself up and out, dripping bloody water onto the deck. "She's gone."

"Is that Vanessa?" Waverly flailed at Archer's back. "Oh my God, how can that be? I was just with her a few minutes ago."

Everyone turned to stare at her then.

"She was...not like this. Alive. Very alive." Waverly paled.

Captain Alex began barking orders over his radio. "I need all hands on Deck Two. Bring any weapons you have. Be on the lookout for suspicious persons heading away from the pool area."

He looked to his officer then. "Ted, grab the log book from the office. I want to verify every gun we have onboard against it. Immediately. Check each one to see if it's been fired since last cleaning."

They had several, for safety in sometimes dangerous parts of the world.

"While you're in there, download the camera feeds for the past fifteen minutes. Put them in the officers' shared folder and be prepared to forward them to the authorities when I have more information."

"Yes, sir," Ted answered before running toward the interior of the ship.

"Archer?" Waverly seemed dazed.

He faced her then, pressing her to his chest so she couldn't keep staring at the dead body.

Tosin assigned himself to crowd control, corralling the guests away from the area while keeping them together for their safety. It also prevented anyone from leaving before they could be questioned.

Captain Alex approached the pool and knelt, carefully retrieving a two-liter bottle from its surface with gloved hands and setting it aside. "Whoever did this knew what they were doing. They silenced the shot with this."

"Explains why we didn't hear anything." Banks grimaced. "We were right up there, though it is quite windy tonight."

Archer thought back to how they'd had to pin down their papers.

"There's a storm coming. I'm going to call this in." Captain Alex frowned. "Closest port is Kralendijk. They'll probably have us dock as planned so they can conduct an investigation."

"Who would do this? Why?" Waverly trembled in Archer's hold.

Those were very good questions. He wondered if she was also thinking about the fact that they were trapped onboard with a killer. No matter how much he rubbed her arms in an attempt to warm them, she shivered harder. Banks appeared with a blanket. Together they wrapped her up.

Miguel stood nearby, not saying anything. Quietly, he observed everything and everyone around them.

It wasn't long before Ted returned carrying a binder. He set it on a nearby table, grabbed one of the four thousand tabs on the side, and opened it. Crew members lined up to present their weapons. He swabbed the inside of each one with a Q-tip before confirming it was clean and checking it off the list.

When everyone had made it through the line, he slapped his hand flat on the table. "Damn it. That's all of them."

"Well, it wasn't a ghost that put a hole in that woman's head." Captain Alex turned an unhealthy shade of purple.

Archer thought he might only be a couple of hues behind.

"Excuse me...sir?" Ted seemed almost afraid. "I know of another weapon onboard. Not listed here."

"Whose is it?" Captain Alex demanded.

Ted pointed. Directly at Waverly. "She had it in Caracas. When we ran from those thugs. And she damn well knew how to use it, too."

Archer growled. Waverly flinched in his grip. "Of course she does. She's a Navy veteran. Waverly had *nothing* to do with this!"

"It's fine, Archer. Sorry, I should have thought of it myself." She separated from him then and turned to the captain. "Yes, I have my weapon. It was cleared by Banks that I bring one."

"Where is it?" the captain asked, not unkindly.

Good, Archer thought. *I won't have to fire his ass.* Ted, however, was on thin ice.

"He's just doing his job." Waverly patted Archer's chest when she realized what he was fuming at. "The gun is in the safe in our room. It's unloaded. Should I go get it?"

"Why don't you stay here?" Miguel said both too quickly, and a little too loudly. "I'll do it. Archer told me the combination earlier because that's where we put...*stuff.*"

He'd almost mentioned their treasure.

Waverly nodded. "Thanks."

Unfortunately, Archer didn't think his friend was motivated entirely by kindness. He'd better knock that shit off fast.

"While we're waiting, let's pull up the camera feeds, Ted," Captain Alex boomed.

The guy looked miserable. Like he'd rather have anything else to say other than, "When I went to download the footage, they weren't running. Looks like they were shut off about an hour ago. Sorry, sir."

"Fuck!" Archer couldn't stand how everything was spiraling out of his control.

Little did he know, it was about to get a whole lot worse.

Miguel stomped back onto the deck. He shouted, "It's gone!"

"My gun?" Waverly put her hand on her chest. Archer cupped her elbow, keeping her upright.

"That too." He kicked a chair over, making a clatter that drew the attention of everyone in sight.

"Oh, shit." Tosin put his head in his hands over where he sat with the guests.

"Does someone want to fill me in on what's going on?" Captain Alex spoke quietly. It was so much more intimidating than if he'd yelled.

Banks shuffled close and spoke low enough that no one else could hear. The captain's eyes grew wide. Then he released a string of curses that impressed Archer with its creativity and pure vileness.

His thoughts exactly.

"I didn't do this!" Waverly wrestled with the blanket, shoving it off. "Swab my hands. Please."

"No. You don't have to do that." Archer's hackles rose.

"She does. We shouldn't assume she's innocent just because you're fucking her," Miguel spat.

Archer's hands balled into fists and he advanced.

Banks stopped him in his tracks. "Let her do it. It will go a long way in clearing her name. We both know there's nothing there."

At least one of them was thinking straight.

Waverly held out her hands. He couldn't help but notice they shook.

Ted zoomed in and used a bunch of the cotton swabs, then put them in a plastic bag and sealed it. At a loss for words, or what to try next, most everyone milled around. Captain Alex pulled Vanessa's emergency contact sheet and passed it to Banks. Waverly groaned when she realized the phone call he'd have to make soon.

Captain Alex gave more orders. "We're going to conduct a room search. Top to bottom of this boat. We're looking for a handgun, or anything else out of place."

Still, Miguel wasn't satisfied. Against everyone's cautioning, he edged nearer. He lowered his voice so only Archer, Banks, and Waverly could hear. "I'm worried for you, bro. You went from believing you raped this girl to chasing her like a puppy dog. She had you wrapped around her ring finger in a matter of days. It looks bad. Let them do this the right way so you don't get any blowback. I know she'd have to be like the world's greatest actress—a master manipulator—to have fooled us all, but..."

He stopped short of mentioning that it might run in her family.

Even that seed of doubt felt like a complete betrayal to Archer. How could his best friend be this disloyal? "She had *nothing* to do with this."

Waverly stared blankly at the two men. She seemed overwhelmed and unable or unwilling to defend herself. So not like her. It infuriated him.

"How can you be so sure? Is this going to be like the time you forgot to mention you were Daddy Warbucks?" Miguel ripped out of Banks's restraining grip on his biceps. "Are you telling us everything you know?"

"Shit! Yes. Guys, I swear. I don't know what's going on, but Waverly isn't to blame." Archer stood tall, wondering if they'd make it past their first destination before their entire future went to hell.

"I'm starting to feel like I don't know who you are anymore," Miguel sneered. "I hope you're not being used. Blind faith doesn't cut it for me. You're already changing who you are for her, staying out of the clubroom. That'll never last. The two of you won't make it if you can't be honest about who you are and what you like."

The sound Waverly made then threatened to rip Archer's heart out of his chest.

She tapped out. "That's it. I'm done. I'll be in our cabin if anyone wants to arrest me. Or make me walk the fucking plank for that matter."

Then she took off. For her to show even a hint of weakness meant they'd really hurt her.

Archer roared, then lunged at Miguel. "Fuck you! She's innocent!"

Before Miguel could take it back or say something to make it worse, Archer shut him up with a punch to the face. Tosin scrambled to Miguel's side and helped him sit up, shaking him from his daze.

Archer and Miguel stared each other down like two groupers defending their territory.

"Enough!" Banks shouted as he smacked his palm on Archer's chest, keeping him from pressing ahead. "What he said about Waverly was out of line. That girl isn't capable of hurting anyone. I know it, same as you. So why don't you go help her instead of making things worse? Captain Alex and I will handle this. In fact, everyone return to your rooms for the night. No one is to be wandering about until I say otherwise. We'll assemble a small team to conduct the searches. Cooperate with all staff instructions. Use your intercoms if you need anything or see something suspicious."

Archer blinked then, thinking about how he'd let Waverly go when there was still a murderer on the loose. He wanted nothing more than to take her into her arms and promise everything was going to be okay.

He spun on his heel. As he strode away, he heard Banks scolding Miguel, "What did I tell you about earning that black eye, huh?"

It might have been funny some other time.

Not with a corpse onboard, though.

Or his woman, falsely accused, nursing some stab wounds in the back.

He jogged the rest of the way to their cabin, ignoring the worried looks everyone shot at him as he passed. Only one person mattered at the moment. Banks and Captain Alex could handle the rest.

When Archer arrived, he found the door unlocked, which only pissed him off more. She should be taking better precautions. Someone had been here. Invaded their personal space once already. His anger transformed into something more desperate when he stood outside the door to the bathroom and heard the sound of weeping, nearly—though not entirely— disguised by the running shower.

It wasn't like Waverly, though she'd softened some since she'd returned to the *Divemaster*. He was sure she would hate for him to see it. So he paced, waiting for her to emerge on her own terms.

He'd be there when she was ready for his open arms.

But it wasn't easy.

In fact, it was one of the hardest things he'd ever done.

For her, he would manage.

"**Y**ou can't blame them for their suspicions, Archer. They're right. This looks bad." Waverly chewed on her fingernail as she stood at the glass accordion doors that led out onto Archer's stateroom balcony. The ocean looked mean and kind of angry as the wind picked up and waves crashed, a storm rolling in. Just when she'd started to feel like she belonged, the world reminded her that anything could be lost in an instant.

She tugged the thin silk robe she'd thrown on after her shower more tightly around her.

Maybe she'd been deluding herself to think this could be her forever. She wasn't a partner in the Divemaster Project. Hell, she wasn't even an owner-operator of her aircraft. Waverly was a simple pilot, working a job, and she'd let herself forget for a while that she could be banished from her new haven as quickly as she had been admitted.

They could fire her over this. Worse, have her thrown in a foreign jail for a murder she didn't commit.

She might not survive losing everything again if it meant Archer went with it.

"I don't give a fuck what it looks like. I've learned my lesson about that shit—believing what people lead you to think. I *know* you had nothing to do with killing that woman and nothing will ever convince me otherwise."

His unwavering faith changed her. Altered everything she felt and opened new doors.

If he was strong enough to have confidence in her after the damage his father had wrought on his impressionable young psyche, she should be able to do the same for him. "Take me to the clubroom. The one the guys were talking about."

"What?" He tipped his chin. "Now? This isn't the time—"

"It is." She put her hand out, waiting for him to take it. "You trust me. And I trust you, too. I know it must be hard to let go of your unnecessary remorse after years of thinking you'd taken advantage of me. I'm guessing *that's* why you didn't tell me about the clubroom. Like Miguel said, if you can't get past that, we'll never last. So we might as well test it out and see before either of us is too invested."

"He's an idiot. He was freaked out and pissed off and not thinking straight."

"That doesn't mean he wasn't right about some of it. Besides, I need this tonight. You. Anything goes. Hell, from now on, that's how it should be. You've given me everything I need and believe in me completely. Allow me the opportunity to do the same for you."

"Waverly..."

"This is *my* choice. I don't want there to be boundaries between us. Limits on our relationship." She drew a deep, somewhat shaky breath. "I can't stand the thought of losing you. You should have told me this is something you need."

"I'm not going anywhere." Archer cursed. "*You* are what I need. I'm sorry the guys questioned you. They'll come around. They're—"

"They're just looking out for you. Totally understandable." Though it had stung, still did, she appreciated their loyalty. "Still, if I'm going to be out of control when it comes to the awful shit in my life, you might as well show me the upside of freefalling."

"What do you mean, Waverly?" He nudged her shoulder until she rotated, facing him. "Look at me when you explain."

He wanted to read the truth in her eyes? Fine by her.

"Ever since...what happened to us all that time ago, I've protected myself by staying in charge. Of myself. Of situations. Of lovers. Not with you, though. I can't do it with you. Don't care to. So take me all the way. Show me what it feels like to give up power. Completely."

There, she'd said it.

"You're sure?" He rubbed her upper arm with the palm of his hand, slowly, comforting.

"Yes. Especially tonight, I don't want to have to think. I just want to feel and experience what you do to me. My brain hurts, my heart hurts. Take all of that away. Fix me. That's what you're into, right?" Could he hear the plea in her voice? She needed this. Needed *him*.

"No, Waverly. I told you, I'm into *you*." Without another word, Archer scooped her into his arms and marched down the hallway to the black glass door she'd wondered about once or twice.

So *that's* what they were hiding in there.

His jaw clenched and unclenched, making his bearded cheeks bulge. Was he second-guessing himself?

"Don't." She stroked the side of his face. "This is what I want."

He lowered her feet to the ground, steadying her before he let go. He used his palm to scan the door open then stepped inside. "If you come in here, it has to be of your own volition."

She stepped across the threshold without hesitation. Going one step further, she unbelted her robe and let the silk slip off her shoulders. It landed in a pile at her feet, leaving her entirely naked.

"Will you wish you hadn't done this tomorrow, after tonight's insanity dies down?" he murmured as he surveyed every inch of her body.

She shook her head, shivering at the feel of her own hair brushing her back. Sensual and liberating, it confirmed his assessment that she should leave it down most times.

"You promised you trust me. So trust me to know my own mind." Waverly tipped her face up and waited for him to accept the invitation.

Archer didn't make her wait long. He laid his lips on hers and slowly ate at her mouth. Her knees went weak and she relied on him to support her, which he did. They stayed that way for a long time, soothing each other with the caress of their lips and tongues.

From far away, Waverly heard a beep. Then another. And a third.

The door rattled as someone tried the handle.

Was one of the other divemasters trying to bring a date to the clubhouse? She hadn't heard of them fooling around with any of the guests, but maybe they were capable of more discretion than she imagined. Or maybe they also needed release after the stress of the evening.

Archer cursed. He settled her on the floor when it was clear she couldn't stand on her own right then. He positioned her so that she was kneeling, sitting on her heels, her hands clasped on her thighs. "Stay right here."

He strode to the door and unlocked it before opening it a crack. Could whoever it was see her? Maybe. Why didn't that bother her as much as it should? In fact, she shifted a little, trying to ease the ache in her core at the thought.

She didn't lift her stare off the ground to find out for sure either way.

"What?" Archer snarled with a venom he'd never aimed at her before. Hopefully, never would. "I'm occupied."

"We wanted to apologize." It was Miguel.

Waverly's earlier stomachache returned.

"You can tell me how stupid you are tomorrow. When I'm not in the middle of something important. Like repairing the damage you caused." Archer didn't add *you idiot*, but his tone said it for him.

There was a pause, and then Tosin said, "We want to apologize to *her*, not you. Let us do it our way. So she knows we're serious and that we do care for her. Anyone this important to you is important to us."

"We fucked up," Miguel admitted to Archer. "Me especially."

At that, Waverly felt something unravel inside her. Her breath caught and a sob escaped before she could clamp her throat down around it. She hugged herself then, rocking to alleviate the sharp stab of pain caused by the sudden snap of tension, which had wound her tight.

They didn't really believe she was a monster like her father. Or Archer's.

"Waverly!" Archer forgot about their visitors and dashed to her side. He crouched by her and wrapped her in his arms. "I've got you. You're okay."

It turned out power exchanges played with her emotions instead of only her body. Who knew?

She was glad she did now, as she experienced a whole new level of intimacy with Archer. "I moved."

"I'll punish you for it later." He smiled as he said it, making her sure she wouldn't find his penalty tortuous in the least. "You heard what they said? That they're dumbasses who should never have doubted you? Not even for the blink of an eye?"

Well, he'd taken some creative license in his paraphrasing, but she didn't argue. Waverly nodded.

"Remember what you said before, about trusting me absolutely?" He drew a long, slow breath.

She nodded again.

"We're about to find out if you meant it." He leaned down to kiss her nose then turned toward the door. "Miguel. Tosin. Get in here and lock that behind you."

If she had said no right then, Archer would have kicked them out in an instant. Knowing that made her comfortable enough not to do it. Even though she was naked and they were not as they eyed her with the same hunger they reserved for the Sunday brunch buffet. Their favorite.

Archer lifted her as if she were a doll. He didn't go far. Just a few strides of his long legs took him to a leather-and-chain contraption that hung from the ceiling. Some sort of sex swing.

She whimpered when he set her down on her back. It moved beneath her, making her prepare for impact with the floor. Waverly wrapped her legs around his waist as if that would save her.

Miguel was there, taking her hand. "We won't let you fall."

He kissed her wrist, testing the waters.

She shivered. So he continued distracting her while Archer strapped a wide belt around her middle. He shook the swing. Chains rattled. Truly secure, she didn't budge.

Meanwhile, Miguel increased his contact, leaving a trail of soft, wet kisses along the inside of her forearm as Archer petted her hip, silently promising it was okay for her to enjoy his friend's attention.

It felt odd to be touched in so many places at once. Even more so when Tosin caressed her leg before prying it off Archer and shackling her ankles to the dangling stirrups. The device was much more comfortable than she would have guessed. It conformed to her, moved with her.

It was surreal, to be the center of attention, surrounded by three smoking-hot men. Especially when they began to strip, letting her watch.

She wasn't about to complain.

"I want you to know," Archer said to her then, "I'm not going to let them fuck you."

She flinched at the thought while his friends groaned their disappointment.

No, she belonged to Archer alone.

"You're mine. But for what they did to you earlier, I'll let them bring you pleasure to replace the pain. I'll let them watch as I do the same so that no one can deny how much you mean to me or how well-matched we are." Archer reached out and inserted two fingers into her soaked pussy.

Going from nothing to something that quickly shocked her system.

If she thought that felt good, it was nothing compared to the arousal that lit up every nerve ending in her body when he withdrew the digits and held them out to Miguel.

Without question, he sucked her flavor off his best friend's hand.

"Shit, she's delicious. Let me taste her while you fuck." She'd never heard Miguel's voice sound so gravelly before. Sexy and rough. He would be most women's fantasy come to life. A passionate Latin lover, committed to pleasing his partner. Thoroughly.

Waverly no longer had the ability to respond. Instead, she watched as Archer directed his friends, and all three of the men worked as a team to shower her with ecstasy.

"Wait until I'm fully buried inside her, then you can play with her clit," Archer told Miguel. "She's extremely responsive and multi-orgasmic. So if you don't have her coming on my cock every couple of minutes, you're not doing a good enough job."

Miguel looked at her reverently. It glued some of the cracks he'd caused in her heart earlier. She'd say their plan was working, because there was no way she could deny their admiration and respect when they treated her like this. Like she was special. Prized. Meant to be worshiped.

Tosin joined the action then when he said to Archer, "Put me in, coach."

Miguel snorted.

"Get to work on her tits. She likes medium-firm pressure. Lots of tongue. Not so much teeth."

It shocked her that he already knew how to play her body that well. She figured it shouldn't since they'd spent a lot of time in bed together these past few weeks, but to hear how finely he'd catalogued her reactions made her glow.

Tosin smiled at her. He brushed his thumb over her lower lip before leaning in. Without making her beg, he plumped her breasts in his hands then took the tip of one into his mouth. He suckled her differently than Archer would have but quickly adapted his style based on the moans and sighs he drew from her with the flickering of his tongue and the suction he applied.

Her eyes kept trying to flutter closed. She fought the temptation so she could burn the image of the three men standing around her into her memory. Though the trio was present, only one directed their union.

Archer.

He was staring down at her as he fisted his cock, preparing it for the fuck of a lifetime.

When their gazes collided, he moved forward, poking her with the tip.

She arched as much as she could in the swing, trying to embed him within her.

A stinging slap landed on her thigh, surprising a shriek out of her. The tingling burn that followed made her wish he'd done it again. Until Archer grabbed the chains holding her legs up and open for him then advanced the last step necessary to slide the fat head of his cock inside her pussy.

At the same time, Tosin switched his skilled handling to her other breast, making her quake.

Archer's well-defined arm muscles bulged, pulling her toward him so that he used her to fuck himself. He hadn't gotten more than the tip of his erection inside her when he stopped, either to let her adjust or to keep himself from getting too fired up too quickly. Could have been both.

"Archer," Miguel warned. "Condom."

"We don't use them." It was another sign of their commitment, she thought.

A declaration of monogamy and confidence. Or foolishness.

She'd certainly never let any other guy fuck her without one.

"Damn," Tosin lifted his mouth from her chest momentarily to groan. "Bareback? I can't wait to see her pussy dripping with your come."

Waverly's muscles clenched at the thought, causing a chain reaction. Archer sank inside her farther. Tosin clung to her nipple even as she rocked, adding more pressure than he had before. And Miguel, refusing to be left out of the mix, bent over so that he could lap her clit while Archer continued to fit himself into her body.

Watching the three men, so close to each other, focused on delivering as much ecstasy as possible, had her poised on the edge of orgasm before they'd even gotten started. As if that wasn't enough to obliterate any remaining self-control she had, someone shocked her by pressing a lube-slicked finger to her ass.

She didn't even know who it belonged to. It didn't matter. It was an extension of Archer.

"Shh, let it in," he coached her, obviously more aware of their surroundings than she was. "You'll like it. I promise. They know what they're doing."

Filled in front and back, with a pair of tongues lashing her most sensitive parts while Archer rode her, it didn't take long for Waverly to reach her breaking point.

"You're going to come for me already?" Archer didn't sound like he was upset about that. "Show them how lucky I am to have you. Go ahead."

Six hands now stroked her, from her arms, which had gotten attached to either side of the leather pillow her head rested on, to her ribs to her calves and everywhere in between. Tongues licked, mouths sucked, and Archer's dick fucked.

And fucked.

And fucked.

Sometime after her fourth or fifth orgasm, Tosin spared her breasts and diverted his attention, at least for a little while. He whispered, "We're sorry, Waverly."

Then he kissed her. Lightly, in contrast to the escalating thrusts of Archer's shaft within her.

In the midst of the passionate tsunami that threatened to wipe her out with a mammoth wall of pleasure, she had an epiphany.

Waverly met Archer's stare as he rammed into her. Sweat poured down his face and chest. She'd never seen him so frantic, or so honest. Was it because his friends were there to make sure he didn't go too far? Or because, for the first time, he planned on ravishing her without stopping short?

Given their history, she figured it was the former.

She realized then that up until this moment he had still been cowering. Running from the negative aspects of his legacy. Too afraid he would become his father—though two men couldn't possibly be more dissimilar—to embrace his wealth, his power, or his dominant streak.

This man unleashed, fully revealed to her for the first time—*this* was Archer.

And she couldn't possibly love him more.

Too bad every cell in her body was focused on complying with his demands or she would have told him so.

Waverly looked at Miguel, then Tosin, hoping they knew how much their apology had meant to her. That went double for the affection they lavished on her. For Archer's friends to so obviously approve of her as his mate, it mattered.

To them all.

"She's getting close again," Miguel warned Archer and Tosin, though she was fairly sure there was no way Archer could miss that fact considering how tightly she gripped his shuttling cock. For that matter, her ass clamped down on the finger buried inside it, too.

Her entire being gathered, compressed like a black hole about to explode in a big bang. She was afraid to surrender to the overwhelming feelings that were inspiring her in case she flew apart and could never pull herself back together again.

"Do it," Miguel urged her. "Let go of it all. Give him everything. It will be okay. We won't let anything happen to you. We're sorry we let you down, Waverly. It won't happen again."

Archer stared at her, unblinking as he pummeled her in a frantic pace.

When she realized that by holding out, she was prolonging his torture, she listened to Miguel.

She surrendered.

The rapture that overtook her then made the whole world seem brighter for an instant. Energy pulsed between her and the three guys who bonded with her. Most of all, with Archer.

She threw her head back, discovering that the ceiling was mirrored.

Waverly studied their reflection as she absorbed the sensations given to her by one man, though he used two additional people to make his gift. The image that came back to her like the hottest porn she'd ever watched multiplied her pleasure.

With one final massive thrust, Archer shattered her.

Waverly came and came and came as she felt him do the same.

The guys got their wish as they watched up close while Archer blasted her with his come, painting her pussy from the inside out. He coated her in his epic release, making Miguel and Tosin curse then shout.

Had they been jerking off? She couldn't see since they knelt beside the swing, their lower bodies out of view. Were they coming too?

She no longer cared, though the thought that witnessing her and Archer's joining could impact them too only made her more shivery inside. She flew, riding the rush that accompanied the best orgasm of her life. When it was over, the three men around her helped her glide back to earth with soft pets and kind words.

Eventually Tosin and Miguel stood to go. They each kissed one of her cheeks before Miguel murmured, "Welcome to the club."

She drifted off then, barely able to stay awake as exhaustion washed over her.

The last thing she remembered was Archer praising her as he collected her and took her back to their room. He tended to her, sitting with her in the hot tub on the balcony for a few minutes so the jets could massage her sore muscles. Then he dried her off and tucked her into their bed. He spooned her as he held tight, refusing to let her go.

If only they could stay that way forever.

Archer must have sensed her slight tensing. He stroked her belly, taking it away again, helping her stay relaxed after the enormous relief he'd granted her. "We'll worry about tomorrow, tomorrow. For now, sleep. I'm with you," he promised before placing an achingly tender kiss on her cheekbone.

Trusting him, as she had promised she did, she sank into his sheltering arms and yielded to unconsciousness.

✹ TWENTY-THREE ✹

Trouble came looking for them before tomorrow could fully become tomorrow.

A triple bang on the door to the owner's suite had Archer sitting upright then rolling from bed in an instant. He hadn't slept long, but he'd slept hard. The best sex of a man's life would do that to him, even if there was trouble as massive as theirs looming.

A glance at the bedside clock confirmed it was two in the morning.

For a split second he thought, *please don't let there be another body*, followed by, *if there is, at least I can be Waverly's alibi this time*. It was an awful thing to think, and made his stomach roil.

When he opened the door, no one was there.

Or at least, not at eye level.

A groan drew his attention to Ted, slumped on the ground. Blood poured from between his fingers, which clutched his abdomen. "Son of a bitch! Waverly, get the doctor!"

Archer whipped off his shirt and pressed it to the gash in the young guy's torso.

In the background he heard Waverly calling for help.

It wasn't long before people rushed them from both sides of the hall. Miguel, Tosin, Banks, Captain Alex, and the doctor huddled around. It only took a look or two for the doctor to say, "I can get him stable, but we don't have blood onboard for a transfusion. He needs to be flown out of here. As quickly as possible."

"Let me get dressed." Waverly ducked back inside long enough to throw on her uniform.

"Is the weather too bad for flying?" Archer asked. "I don't like this."

"I'm not going to let another person die if I can help it." She dared anyone to stop her.

Miguel spoke up. "Hey, don't feel the need to prove something just because I was an idiot before. No one thinks you had anything to do with Vanessa's murder. If this isn't wise, you shouldn't do it."

Ted groaned again, drawing their attention. He seemed less alert.

Captain Alex kept asking him who'd attacked him. He wasn't responding.

"It's the right thing to do," she insisted. "I can fly in this. It's not that long of a flight and I'll be heading away from the storm. The sooner we take off, the better."

Archer wrapped her in a bear hug. "Be safe."

"I promise."

"Come back quick. I've got more things to show you in the clubroom." He kissed her then, branding her with his passion. Or at least he hoped he had.

Then there was less time for talking as people did their jobs. Tosin helped the doctor get Ted situated and into the chopper. Banks called ahead to the hospital and let them know there was a patient en route. Captain Alex spoke with the authorities.

Archer watched as his girlfriend climbed into a helicopter to save someone's life.

She was amazing.

He held his breath as she lifted off and watched until she blended into the darkness. His chest ached when he could no longer make out the blinking lights on the helicopter.

"Let's go to the bridge. That way you can still talk to her until she gets there safe," Miguel offered, nudging Archer inside.

They got there just in time to hear Ted command Waverly, "Turn off the radio."

Archer's spine went ramrod straight. Why would he say that? And why didn't he sound as out of it as he had been a few minutes ago? His condition should deteriorate as he lost more blood, not improve.

A couple of clicks came over the air before Waverly said, "Okay, it's off. What's up?"

Captain Alex acted quickly, mashing a few buttons on his own control panel. "I've muted our end so he thinks she really did it."

If Ted believed that, he would be the stupidest guy on the planet. Then again, there was no faking how much he'd bled. Maybe he was afraid or wanted to make a deathbed confession, just in case. "Good, thanks. We're not going to the hospital. Not to any island, either. Take me back to Caracas. Or someplace else in South America we can reach easily. Anywhere I can rent a car and be on my way. You're the pilot, use your imagination."

Every person on the bridge went quiet. Dead quiet.

"Why should I do that, Ted?"

Archer wondered if he was the only person who could hear the barest hint of fear in Waverly's voice. For her, that was a lot. There was a whole heap of *fuck you* in her tone, too. That scared him to the bone.

"Because I'll split the profits from selling these with you." A rustle, and then a pause.

"Where did you get a giant ruby and a bunch of gold coins?" Waverly asked, clearly letting them know what was happening.

"NO!" Archer shouted as he swiped his arm across the table. He sent papers, glasses, instruments, and who knew what else crashing to the floor. This couldn't be happening.

His nostrils flared. He had to do...something, anything, but there was no way to reach Waverly. He couldn't intervene or assist. Helpless, all he could do was listen.

"Let's call it a parting gift from your boyfriend. I found them in his safe after I overheard him telling Miguel the combination this morning. Saved me a step. I was going for the gun so I could take you hostage and maybe get some ransom money out of him. I mean, I know that didn't exactly work out the first time I tried it, back in Caracas, but first I didn't think he gave a shit about you. And then when they said he was on his way, those assholes took forever showing up. How did I know your boyfriend was going to get there so damn quick? He must really like you. Which is great for getting top dollar. But this...this is way easier." He laughed then, and it was clear he might be a couple rubies short of a necklace himself.

"So what's in it for me?"

"I'll give you a cut. How's thirty percent?"

"Why shouldn't I haul you back to the *Divemaster* and collect a reward the honest way?" she asked.

"Don't antagonize the wackadoodle, Waverly!" Banks shouted, though he knew she couldn't hear him.

Ted didn't say anything to that.

But Waverly did. "Oh. Well, I guess that answers the question about where my gun went."

Archer couldn't breathe, couldn't see. Miguel and Tosin were there, holding him steady.

"If I'm crazy enough to stab myself to get airlifted to South America, I'm crazy enough to use this." No one would argue with him about that. "If Vanessa hadn't seen me coming out of your room and ran off to tattle, I wouldn't have had to shoot her. Then I could have waited until tomorrow and taken off before anyone knew this stuff was missing. The room searches were getting closer. I couldn't take any more chances. I've never done anything like this before. I don't particularly like it either. Couldn't stand it on that ship, being ordered around, nowhere to go to get away and no other skills to earn a living. What good is a ship's officer who doesn't want to live on ships? It was driving me nuts. I need a way out. This is it. Sometimes you do what you have to in order to survive, right?"

"Right. I know exactly what you mean," she said.

Captain Alex muttered something about background checks. There hadn't been any dirt to find. Archer didn't blame him, or Banks, or anyone except Ted himself for this disaster.

"I'd like my gun back now, Ted." Waverly sounded calm and almost friendly, though Archer knew she was seething inside.

"Um, how about no?" the punk answered.

"We both know that as soon as I land this helicopter, I'm of no use to you. What's to keep you from shooting me then?" she asked.

Archer was wondering the same thing, and he couldn't imagine this ending well.

In the background he heard Captain Alex calling in an update to the authorities. Why bother? There was nothing they could do either. Waverly was the only one who had even a bit of control over her future right now.

And he didn't like her odds.

Ted didn't answer again.

"Look..." Waverly tried another tactic. "You're bleeding really heavily still. You're going to need help to get fixed up. Give me the gun, and I'll take it as a good faith gesture that you'll keep your word on splitting the cash from the treasure. I'll help you hide from Archer and back you up when the doctors ask where you got that gash."

It said something that no one in the bridge reacted to her faux-bargain. Not a single person believed she would actually do that to him. Archer especially.

"Just fly, bitch."

"If that's the way you want it." Waverly sighed. Then whispered, "I love you, Archer."

"That's sweet. But your boyfriend isn't here to save you."

"That's okay. I've got this," she said.

Right before a gunshot rang out and the communications with the chopper failed for real.

Archer didn't care who heard—he howled, the sound tearing out of him like someone had ripped his soul from his chest. He crashed to his knees, unable to stand.

Everyone else in the room was still as statues, frozen by shock at what they'd just heard.

Not Archer. He went ballistic. "We've got to find her! What are her coordinates?"

Someone called out the final reading before everything had gone dark.

"It'll take a few hours for the ship to get over there given the tides and this current, if we can even make it with the weather escalating and nighttime to contend with. We could run aground. I don't advise attempting it before dawn, if at all." Captain Alex closed his eyes briefly. "In fact, I *can't* do it. There are other people's lives at stake on this ship. They're my responsibility. I'm sorry."

Miguel stepped up then. "Come on, Archie. We'll take the Zodiac."

"Is that prudent?" Banks asked, utter devastation twisting his features into an unrecognizable mask.

Captain Alex said, "No."

At the same time, Archer, Tosin, and Miguel said, "Yes."

"Wait." Banks tried again. "Let's think. Another senseless death, or three, isn't going to bring her back."

"Don't talk like that! Like she's gone!" It couldn't be. Archer continued, "I'll drop dead of a heart attack anyway if I have to sit on my hands for hours to find out what's happened to her. She could be hurt. Without help, she might...no. I can't take that chance. I wouldn't be able to live with myself."

"I said it wasn't smart. But I won't stop you." Captain Alex admitted, "It's what I would do if she was my girlfriend."

So it was decided.

"Be careful, boys." Banks did something Archer had never seen him do in all his life. He sank to his knees and began to pray.

The three divemasters slammed out the door and into the pouring rain. They prepped the boat without bothering to shout above the wind. Then they strapped themselves into life jackets. Just before they climbed in, the thing bucking so hard they clipped themselves to it with lines and carabiners, Archer turned to them. "This is crazy. I should go alone."

"No way," Miguel said immediately. "You can handle the navigation and the driving solo, but you can't reach the spotlights from back there. Without those, you won't make it more than a quarter mile before you're lost or hit something on the surface and put a hole in this thing."

"You're wasting time," Tosin agreed. "We're doing this together.

With that, they launched the boat and took off, leaving the relatively safety and ultimate comfort of the *Divemaster* behind them, possibly for the last time.

Archer had never been so scared in his life.

Not because of the waves, or the storm…

But because he didn't know what he would find when they reached Waverly's final transmitted coordinates.

It was the longest thirty-five minutes of his life.

The rough ocean tossed the guys around like a rubber ducky in a whirlpool.

They'd circled the area Waverly had last radioed from at least a dozen times and didn't see her anywhere. He wasn't sure what he'd expected but was starting to feel foolish. It was entirely possible that his rash decision could get them all killed.

He refused to think about the possibility that Waverly was already waiting for them below the surface.

Every bit of him hurt.

"Archer, I hate to say this," Miguel shouted from up front. "But...I think we've got to call it for the night. It's getting rougher. We're in trouble. I don't even think we should try to make it back."

Tosin didn't say anything. Instead, he nodded, looking green.

"Fuck!" Archer yelled, then admitted defeat. "You're right. Find someplace to beach this thing and ride the storm out. We can start searching again as soon as it's clear."

In his mind, he apologized to Waverly for giving up. *I'm sorry. We tried our best. Hang on. Please, don't you quit, too.*

୧୬ TWENTY-FOUR ୧୬

"**I**t's okay. I've got this." Waverly hoped her bravado eased the agony Archer was likely suffering while listening in on this conversation.

If she was going to have any hope of surviving this, shit was about to get even more fucked up than it already was. Before giving Ted too much time to consider what she might be up to, she lashed out with her right hand, grabbing for the gun.

BANG!

Waverly had never been shot before.

It hurt like a motherfucker.

Nothing like in the movies. Adrenaline didn't do shit to numb the blinding pain. Fortunately, it appeared that the bullet had hit her upper left arm. She didn't need that to clobber Ted, who seemed stunned by the reverberations of the deafening blast in such a small space.

More good news, she wasn't dead.

Waverly lashed out, fueled by pure rage and indignation. She punched him where it would hurt most—in the stab wound he'd given himself. Judging by the amount of blood on the bandage, he might have done a better job of that than he'd intended.

Which might have been why he didn't react fast enough to stop her.

With an *oomph*, he dropped the gun.

Waverly didn't pause to think about what she was doing. Survival instincts and her military training kicked in. She snatched the gun, put her finger on the trigger, pointed it straight between Ted's eyes, and squeezed. Twice.

To be honest, she didn't even feel bad about his brains splattered on the window.

If it was her or him, she knew which one she would pick. All day long.

Unfortunately, the gunshots had damaged more than her flesh.

When she tried to radio the *Divemaster* to let Archer know she was okay and about to come home, the damn thing wouldn't work. In the next few seconds, instruments started going dark. Fuck. One of their bullets, or maybe bits of all three, had clipped some important shit.

If it wasn't for the storm, which seemed to have intensified, she might have tried to find her way to the *Divemaster* without some of those tools. Over open ocean, with nowhere to put down quickly, and—oh, yeah—blood slicking her arm, there was no way she was risking it.

Waverly groaned as the pain intensified. She scrunched her eyes closed a few times, trying to see better. In range, a blip of an island with a wide, flat beach beckoned her. It was going to have to do.

It was her worst landing ever.

Later, she couldn't even recall most of it. Though she wasn't really a religious person, she might have believed she had a guardian angel helping out.

But when she turned off the engine, she was down in mostly one piece.

For a while she just sat there and stared. Thanked every power in the universe for helping her save herself. Then she prepared to rough it for a while. No one was going to be able to reach her tonight.

She debated sleeping in the helicopter, but it was pretty exposed on the beach and if it toppled, or sank into the sand as the tides changed, she could be trapped and drown. Given the state of her arm, she couldn't wrestle Ted's body out anyway. The thought of sharing the space with him all night long...

So much nope. Not happening.

Waverly tried to get the radio going one more time without success. So she grabbed the first aid kit and her backpack, then jumped out of the pilot's seat.

She trudged up the beach far enough to huddle at the base of a thick copse of trees. First she treated herself as best she could, using strips of bandages and thick gauze pads—thank you, Ted—to put pressure on her wound without going full-on tourniquet. Her military days had made her aware that she could do permanent damage if she left one of those on for longer than two hours, and it was going to be several times that before help arrived.

They couldn't reach her, never mind find her, in these conditions.

She didn't think her arm was bleeding enough to be life-threatening. Then again, if she passed out and couldn't make a tourniquet once it turned for the worse, saving her arm wouldn't really matter, now would it?

Hard decisions.

After she'd patched it up as best she could and applied the most pressure she felt comfortable with leaving on long-term, she took the Mylar thermal survival blanket out of the first aid kit and wrapped it around herself. A fire was out of the question given the rain and wind, but it wasn't particularly cold out. This would do.

Comfortable? Not especially.

Survivable? Hell yes.

To keep herself from throwing a pity party, she used her teeth to tear open a pack of dried fruit then chugged an entire bottle of water, hoping her body got busy replacing some of her lost blood pretty damn quick.

She estimated she'd been out there less than an hour when she wondered how she would survive an entire night without going bonkers.

Waverly used her good arm to collect the fallen palm fronds she could reach without jostling her injury too much and began to stack them up. She wasn't cold, but it made her feel more secure to have some barrier, however flimsy, between herself and the storm.

When she'd run out of resources, she rested up against the tree trunk that formed one support for her lean-to shelter and wondered how she'd pass the rest of the time. Maybe she could write Archer love letters in the sand. Or draw pictures of positions she wanted to try fucking in once she had healed.

Before she could, a light glinted in her eyes.

Something painfully bright after the deep midnight she had gotten used to.

It was only there for a second, then gone.

Then it came back. And stuck.

Could it be a searchlight?

Holy shit!

Waverly stood up, using the Mylar around her as a reflector. She ran toward the surf then, making it about halfway before a familiar gray rigid hull inflatable boat beached itself on the sand with a landing nearly as poor as hers had been in the helicopter.

She gave it a four out of ten, at best. It was the most wonderful thing she'd ever seen.

Until Archer came flying over the side, tearing up the beach toward her.

Then *that* was the most wonderful thing she'd ever seen.

She supposed they could have cried, flung themselves at each other, or any other number of things. Instead, they stood there, about a foot apart, wind whipping their clothes and hair, grinning like fools.

"Imagine meeting you here," Archer said before his face darkened. "Ted?"

She shook her head. "Dead."

Then he closed the gap between them and crushed her to him.

"I've never been so relieved in my entire life to see someone," he said. "It might be best if I never let you go again."

She was good with that, too. Except just then his arm knocked into hers, right over her bullet wound.

Waverly cried out, wishing she could take it back when worry rushed back to his face. "Arm. Ouchy."

She tried to smile as she winced, probably looking totally weird.

"Is it broken?" he asked. In the meantime, he checked out the helicopter. It perched on the beach, a little wonky, but obviously not crashed.

She knew he was estimating the likelihood she had internal injuries. "No. Shot."

"What?" he yelled.

"Shot."

"And you're *just now* mentioning it?" He tore the thermal blanket off her as if he was making sure she didn't have any other new holes. "Jesus, woman."

There was more blood there than she'd realized. Yikes.

Miguel and Tosin hauled the boat toward them, out of reach of the waves and wind. Exhausted, and stumbling, they began to set it down, even as they told her over and over how glad they were to see her. Tosin used his shoulder and upper arm to wipe moisture from his face. Probably just spray from the ocean. That had to have been an uncomfortable ride.

"I have a camp started over there." She pointed with her good arm, so they angled toward her spot. Archer wasn't having any of that. He plucked her from the beach and carried her. Resting her head on his shoulder, she admitted to herself that she was grateful for the lift.

As they neared the tree line and the wind and rain subsided, she shouted over the crashing waves, "I can't believe you got in that thing with the ocean looking like that! Are you fucking crazy?"

"Well, I had something to say to you that couldn't wait until morning."

"What's that?" She blinked up at him.

"I love you, too, Waverly."

And *that* was the thing that broke her. Tears rolled down her cheeks as he set her on the ground between his best friends. He kissed her with the barest brushes of his lips while Miguel and Tosin propped the boat up on its side, using the wind itself to hold it in place, making a very effective wall against the storm.

With that done, Miguel started pulling things from inside it.

He combined their first aid kits, taking a needle and thread, some topical anesthetic, and a packet of antibiotics from inside. Tosin handed Archer the waterproof radio. "Why don't you do the honors?"

The four of them huddled around the communications device.

"Banks!" Archer shouted.

"Archie! Are you okay?" he asked.

"Yes. We've got her. Waverly's here. She's alive! We've got her!" He beamed at her as if he couldn't believe how lucky they'd gotten.

A riot of claps, whistles, and cheers came over the radio, making Waverly shed a few more fat tears before dashing them away with the back of her hand. To know that she'd gone from being absolutely alone in the world to having this incredible group of people who loved her...

It was everything.

With these guys, she wasn't afraid to let her feelings loose either. They wouldn't judge her or take advantage of her temporary weakness.

Tosin piped up then, his sandy hair looking crazier than she'd ever seen it. "No, she's not just alive. She's sitting here under a palm frond shelter living it up while we all worried about her. Might as well have happened upon her sipping a piña colada."

"Is she wounded?" Captain Alex asked.

"Yup," Miguel confirmed. "Took a bullet to the arm. No biggie, according to her. Honestly, it does look like a flesh wound. We're about to see if I can stitch it up without passing out."

It was crazy how a few near death experiences made these things seem inconsequential. Except… "Guys. Someone else is shot, and this time I *did* do it. I killed Ted."

"You protected yourself," Archer corrected her.

Nobody contradicted him.

She sighed.

"We'll be there as soon as we can get the ship closer or dispatch another helicopter from somewhere," Captain Alex assured them. "The worst of the storm should be past now. Will you be okay until morning?"

"Absolutely," Waverly answered.

"As long as I have her, I'm good." Archer didn't care if it made him sound like a pussy. It was true.

❧ TWENTY-FIVE ❧

Waverly stood at the rail of the main deck of the *Divemaster* as Captain Alex and the harbor pilot navigated them safely out of Kralendijk. They'd dropped off the guests, who would take the Banks Foundation's private jets back to their regularly scheduled lives. Despite the events of the past few days, the passengers had assured them the initial run of the program had been a success.

Part of her was still raw, and probably would be for a while. Her new family here onboard the ship was doing their best to help her forget and move forward. In time, she would.

"I really do love this place," Archer sighed from beside her as he said goodbye to the island that had been his home for a little while.

"At least this time goodbye doesn't have to be forever." Miguel put his hand on Archer's shoulder and squeezed. "We can always come back."

Waverly thought about how she'd returned to Archer and couldn't agree more.

Banks nodded at the guys from where he stood on Waverly's other side. "If there are any special requests, just let me know and I'll adjust the schedule."

"Where are we heading next, anyway?" Tosin wondered. It didn't matter much to them so long as they were together and doing what they loved.

"Eventually, we'll sail to the Panama Canal and out to the Pacific for a while. The season is right over there for great diving," Banks said. "But first we're going to take a detour up to the US Virgin Islands, where the planes will meet us with our next round of passengers in a week or so. It'll be a nice break for the crew. I think everyone could use a few days off."

They all seconded that.

"Am I the only one who's never been before? I've heard it's beautiful." Waverly smiled at Archer, excited to investigate a new place with him. Hopefully one that didn't involve almost getting killed. But did involve lots and lots more of the mind-blowing sex they'd been having since he'd introduced her to the clubroom. Or underwater sex. Or ultra-romantic sex.

Or just plain sex in general.

He'd officially turned her into a sex fiend.

"It is," Archer assured her. "Sorry, though, I need you to do some boring business stuff with me when we get there. After that's done, I'll take you on a sightseeing tour if you want before we have to start the next trip."

"What kind of business stuff?" Something about the way he'd said it tipped her off.

Banks encouraged Archer to continue when he paused. "Go ahead, tell her."

"As partners in the Banks Foundation's Divemaster Project, we've agreed. You deserve a reward for how you handled the situation last week. So Banks helped me buy a new helicopter. An upgrade. A six-seater Eurocopter EC 155."

"Oh my God." Waverly thought that might be better than sex. "I've always wanted to fly one of those."

Archer spilled the beans. "We're picking her up at the Henry E. Rohlsen Airport on St. Croix. And...she's yours."

"What?" Waverly might have jerked away if he hadn't had his arms around her.

"You're free." He smiled softly. "To be honest, from the beginning it didn't sit right that you were tethered here, to me, by the thing that allows you to do what you love most. If you stay—and God, I hope you will—I want it to be because this is where you belong. Where you *choose* to be."

"I..." She couldn't believe what he was saying, or that he might think she felt obligated to remain in his presence. A helicopter, especially one like that, was a ridiculous thing to just give someone. With the chopper itself, she could open a charter business, using the income to cover the operating costs and still make a healthy living. "I don't have anything to give you that could compare to that. Except—"

"I don't need anything in return." He stole a quick kiss, trying to shush her attempts at fairness. "Your happiness is all I ask for."

"What if I want to give you my heart?" Waverly swallowed hard but continued. There was no going back now. "Hell, Archer. You've had it all along. I hope that's enough."

"It's everything," he whispered, his hand trembling where it rested on her neck. "I love you, Waverly."

"I love you, too." It felt so good to say it out loud. She had nearly worn out the words since he'd appeared on that beach to save her ass. She intended to keep being obnoxious about it, too.

"So you'll stay? Let us hire you as an independent contractor. Will you keep traveling the world and hanging out with these crazy shitheads, too?" He waved at his friends and Banks, who were grinning like fools.

"Hell yes!" she shrieked as she flung herself into his arms.

They kissed and kissed while the divemasters cheered them on, until Banks cleared his throat.

"Oh. Hi, Banks. Are you still here? Sorry." Waverly blinked as she returned to reality, hopefully only for as long as it would take Archer to lug her off to their cabin.

"There's one other thing I need you four to do while we're there. The lawyer has contracts for another arm of the Banks Foundation that's been recently established. It will be responsible for the salvage and protection of artifacts from shipwrecks. The organization's first order of business is to retrieve the treasure you discovered. So it's only fitting that you be joint owners of the venture. Early estimates based on the data we sent in say this wreck alone could be worth eight hundred million dollars, give or take. I'd recommend refinancing the next excursion with the profits then splitting the rest between you equally. There will be plenty to go around. Operating expenses for a chopper can be astronomical."

Waverly knew the kind older man was looking out for her, more than her blood relatives ever had. He loved Archer like his own son. And since it seemed that *Archie* was really into her, she had no doubt Banks was finding ways to make her feel like an equal in his company.

An asset instead of a freeloader.

The last of her anxieties eased. She would be forever grateful.

"Thank you," she murmured, then squirmed from Archer's hold to kiss Banks on the cheek.

"You are so very welcome." He hugged her then. Maybe it was possible that after all this time they had managed to shake off the lingering effects of their shady beginnings, and triumph.

Every bit of good the Banks Foundation wrought blasted shadows from the world one by one. She was proud and thrilled to be part of bringing sunshine to people living in the darkness any way possible, seeing as she'd once been a night dweller herself.

Waverly couldn't wait to see where life would take them next, or in ten years. The only thing she knew for sure was that wherever it might be, Archer would be with her.

"I love you," he whispered again while he hugged her tight, as if she might forget.

Sailing off into the sunset with him was as magnificent as she'd always dreamed it would be.

Only, she had never imagined that would be the start of their adventure, not the end of it.

Don't Miss The Rest Of The Divemasters Series!

Going Deep, Divemasters Book 2
Coming June 14th, 2016

When her mentor is killed in a lab fire, all his notes destroyed with him, marine biologist Sabine Reynolds is determined to finish his work—a cure for an aggressive form of cancer. She needs a specific coral to continue. To find it, she boards The Divemaster to search the waters around Hawaii.

Crewmember Miguel Torres helps facilitate the collection…and brings out a sensual side of Sabine she hadn't known existed. In the warm tropical waters, she discovers fascinating things about herself and the taboo fantasies she'd never experienced before meeting the sexy guide, who isn't afraid to take charge during their daytime, and nighttime, adventures.

The Divemaster crew come face-to-face with danger in the form of rival researchers, who'll stop at nothing to ensure their success at Sabine's expense. Sabotage, theft, kidnapping, murder, whatever it takes to produce—and profit from—the cure first.

Can Miguel keep Sabine safe and by his side? Or will her enemies put a stop to her research…permanently?

**Going Hard, Divemasters Book 3
Coming July 12th, 2016**

As the last lone wolf of The Divemaster, Tosin Ellis doesn't plan on partnering up anytime soon. Then his friend Archer commissions an engagement ring for his fiancée…

Jeweler Kahori Akama is sensual, intriguing, and happy to accept Tosin's help sourcing the black pearls she uses in her popular pieces. As their relationship goes from professional to personal, Tosin also learns Kahori's family in under the threat of a blackmailer, someone intent on ruining her father's resort business to lay claim to its valuable property.

Tosin never expected to find a single woman that could slake his sexual appetites, but Kahori surrenders to her raw and primal urges with the natural power of a typhoon strong enough to blow even a veteran sailor far off course. Once he's experienced loving in the eye of the storm, he can't imagine being satisfied by less.

Once more, the crew of The Divemaster will do what it takes to protect their own. Especially Tosin, who realizes Kahori's heart just may be his home.

ABOUT THE AUTHOR

Jayne Rylon is a *New York Times* and *USA Today* bestselling author. She received the 2011 RomanticTimes Reviewers' Choice Award for Best Indie Erotic Romance.

Her stories used to begin as daydreams in seemingly endless business meetings, but now she is a full-time author, who employs the skills she learned from her straight-laced corporate existence in the business of writing. She lives in Ohio with two cats and her husband, the infamous Mr. Rylon.

When she can escape her purple office, Jayne loves to travel the world, SCUBA dive, take pictures, avoid speeding tickets in her beloved Sky and—of course—read.